CLONES vs. Aliens

CLONES vs. Aliens

THE CLONE CHRONICLES #4

M.E. CASTLE

EGMONT
Publishing
New York

EGMONT
We bring stories to life

First published by Egmont Publishing, 2015
443 Park Avenue South, Suite 806
New York, NY 10016

Copyright © Paper Lantern Lit, 2015

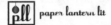 paper lantern lit

1 3 5 7 9 8 6 4 2

www.egmontusa.com
www.theclonechronicles.com

Library of Congress Cataloging-in-Publication Data

Castle, M. E.
Clones vs. aliens / M.E. Castle.
pages cm. — (The Clone chronicles ; #4)
Summary: Twelve-year-old Fisher Bas and his clone work together to save the
world after aliens disguised as twelve-year-old girls invade their town.
ISBN 978-1-60684-534-9 (hardcover)
[1. Cloning—Fiction. 2. Extraterrestrial beings—Fiction. 3. Twins—Fiction. 4.
Bullies—Fiction. 5. Middle schools—Fiction. 6. Schools—Fiction. 7. Science fiction. 8. Humorous stories.] I. Title. II. Title: Clones versus aliens.

PZ7.C2687337Ckv 2015
[Fic]—dc23

2014033763
ISBN 978-1-60684-535-6 (ebook)

Printed in the United States of America

For my Grandma Martha,
Who showed me every summer
That the simplest gestures of love
Leave the deepest impressions.

CLONES vs. Aliens

≋ CHAPTER 1 ≋

I walked into school one morning and destroyed a math test. I walked into school the next day and destroyed the school.   —Fisher Bas, Journal

"One . . . more . . . piece . . . ," Fisher Bas said. Sweat beaded on his forehead. His breathing slowed to near hibernation levels, his hand shifted tremblingly into place. It was Friday afternoon, the end of the school week, and most kids were already on their way home. He, however, had one task left. An outdoor project of unprecedented scope. He was a single piece away from completing what was without a doubt his greatest feat of engineering.

Click.

With the gentle sound of a final, perfect connection slotting home, it was done. Fisher stepped back carefully, shading his eyes against the sun. It truly was a wonder of geometric achievement, a proud symbol of humanity's eternal struggle against gravity.

It was the world's largest freestanding structure built entirely out of King of Hollywood Spicy Star Fry boxes— and would, Fisher hoped, serve as the basis for Wompalog's most impressive Thanksgiving float.

"It's beautiful," breathed Alex, Fisher's clone. Or, to be more specific, his first and least evil clone.

Two weeks earlier, Fisher's second and *very* evil clone, Three, had attempted to take over the city with an army of androids that all looked identical to Fisher. He had very nearly succeeded. In the final showdown, the Wompalog school building had been utterly wrecked. So for now, school was a bunch of trailers hauled into the massive parking lot surrounding the King of Hollywood—which meant constant access to the mind-numbingly delicious fries, and lots of time during lunch to fiddle around with their packaging.

For the first time in a long time, Fisher was relaxed. Thanksgiving was next week. And better, Dr. X was in jail. Three was in the most secure custody the FBI could arrange for minors. Veronica was happy with Fisher. And Alex was his own person instead of a dark secret.

Fisher and Alex had been through an awful lot together in the few short months of Alex's life, whether saving the world from Dr. X, freeing Palo Alto from Three's clutches, or devising a method to trick their dad's genetically engineered cookie-sniffing mongoose when she came into Fisher's room unannounced.

Unless something fell out of the sky in the next few days, then finally, *finally,* Fisher could take it easy for a little while.

Fisher's ears perked up.

"Do you hear something?" he said to Alex.

"Like what?" Alex said.

"Like a hiss, or a whine, or a . . . " Fisher turned, horrified. *Oh, no.* " . . . squeal."

With a resounding oink, a fuzzy, pointy-eared pink missile careened right through Fisher's fry box tower and into Fisher's arms. Fisher tumbled backward with such force that he crashed into Alex, and the three of them—boys and pig—sank into the pile of toppled boxes.

Flying Pig, Alex and Fisher's pet, was a loyal and lovable creature who also seemed to be, aside from a black hole or a gamma ray burst, the single most destructive force in the universe.

After a minute or two of awkward clawing, Fisher's head finally breached the surface of the cooking oil-scented heap.

"Tell me you at least got a picture," he said to Alex. "That was a week of work."

Alex's arm popped up from beneath the cardboard tide, phone clutched in his fist.

"Thank Higgs," Fisher said, hauling Alex out of the wreckage of his masterpiece. "I would've had to reassemble it with glue before mounting it on the float, anyway. The important thing is that we've got the photo to guide us."

FP emerged from the pile a few seconds later, a

Plans for
Spicy Fry Box
Parade Float

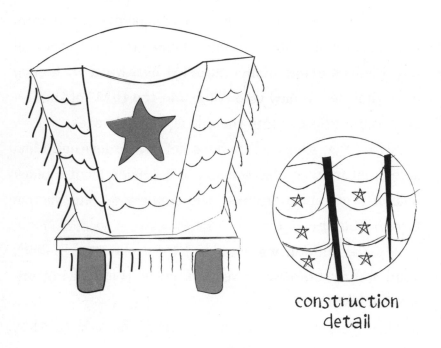

construction
detail

grease-stained box hanging from each ear.

"It's two thirty," Alex said, dusting the oily remains of fry residue from his shoulder. "Time to head home. Maximizing our time away from Wompalog would be optimal."

"I know," Fisher said. "I wrote the equation."

The pleasant residential area Fisher and Alex passed through on the way home showed barely any indication that it had, briefly, been the victim of a hostile android takeover. FP sniffed happily at well-maintained hedges. There weren't any scorch marks or car wrecks, no burned gears or other robotic debris. It looked like any other ordinary neighborhood, where decent people led happy lives and did not have to deal with mechanical armies commanded by under-five-foot tyrant clones.

Fisher breathed easily, hoping it would stay that way at least until the new year. That didn't seem like so much to ask, really.

At the end of their short walk, the Bas home came into view. It was, in fact, very difficult to miss. A cluster of antennae sprang from the roof, transmitting, receiving, and collecting data from dozens of experiments. Mrs. Bas's garden was visible from more than a block away, mostly because of the massive cornstalk that jutted higher than the house. Mr. Bas had named it Fee, as in Fi Fo Fum.

"Tomorrow's going to be fantastic," Fisher said. "Loopity Land will be the biggest thing in town since the first King of Hollywood opened."

"I'm still shocked that our parents helped design an amusement park," Alex said. "I mean, I could see Dad putting together a roller coaster for marmosets or flatworms or something, but entertaining *people*? New territory."

"It's true," Fisher said thoughtfully. The Bas's Liquid

Door front gate, as dense as lead when sitting idle, reduced itself to a vapor-like state as it recognized Alex and Fisher's DNA, allowing them to pass through. "Our parents might be geniuses, but their social skills are definitely remedial."

Mr. and Mrs. Bas had announced earlier in the week that they had secretly been working for over a year on a vast amusement park that was at last nearing completion. Tomorrow, Saturday, would be a trial run to which only the designers and builders were invited.

Fisher, however, had other plans. He'd engineered a special hovering pickpocket drone. If it worked correctly, it would secretly float up behind his parents after they'd entered the park, slip the special entrance passes from their pockets, and deliver them right back to Fisher.

"We're home!" Alex said as he pushed open the front door, which didn't change shape or scan people for DNA because it was just a regular door made of wood. *No need to reinvent the wheel*, Mrs. Bas always said—which was a slightly confused philosophy, since she had, in fact, reinvented the wheel. Three times.

"Hey, boys!" their dad said from the landing halfway down the stairs. "Welcome ho—oooooooooo—" He was interrupted mid-greeting by one of his more recent genetic experiments, Paul, the walking octopus, who had just wrapped himself around Mr. Bas's ankles. Paul had lungs as well as gills, and two extra tentacles that were strong enough to let him glide around on the floor.

With a loud *thunk*, Mr. Bas and Paul landed in a tangled heap at the bottom of the stairs. Paul's tentacles waved in panic as he wiggled underneath Mr. Bas. Fisher was grateful he had recently installed shock-absorbing, impact-reducing stairs. Living with his parents, and his dad in particular, had made them an obvious invention to pursue.

Walter Bas rolled over so Paul could slip out from underneath him. The good-natured cephalopod freed himself, shaking his tentacles out and rubbing his bulbous head. FP stepped up and sniffed at Paul curiously. He was still getting used to having the strange animal around. Paul gave FP a little pat on the snout, and the pig gave a friendly snort.

"Getting into the roller coaster spirit a little early, huh?" said Alex, helping their dad up.

"I guess I am," Mr. Bas said, chuckling a little as he straightened up. "Tomorrow's the big day!"

"I can't wait to see it," Fisher said, feeling the gentle pressure of Paul's many-armed hello on his left calf.

"Unfortunately, you'll have to, at least for a little bit," Mr. Bas said sternly, adjusting his glasses on his nose. Fisher felt Alex's sideways look. "There are a lot of things we need to test before the park can open to visitors," Mr.

Bas went on. "We won't be certain everything is safe and working properly until at least a week of trials have been done. *Especially* on the M3."

Fisher's heart skipped. The M3. Short for Mega Mars Madness. Soon to be the greatest roller coaster in existence. His parents had finally relented and showed Fisher the architectural plans they'd drawn up for its completion. The M3 was so complex even Fisher didn't fully understand it. All he knew was that the beauty of the physics of it overwhelmed him.

Fisher had never been on a roller coaster before; he'd always been too scared. But no more. Maybe it was the influence Alex had had on him. Fisher was still scared, there was no doubt about it. He was just less willing to let fear stop him.

"Of course, we understand," Fisher said, smiling nervously and nudging Alex with an elbow. "We can be patient. It's only a week, after all."

"Boys! I had no idea you were home. Is it three o'clock already? I haven't even had lunch," said Mrs. Bas, stepping in from the living room with a small beaker in her hand. She tapped the beaker a couple of times with a fingernail. "You know how time flies when I'm working on something. Well, I'd better get back to testing this project."

"What is it?" asked Fisher, stepping forward to get a better look. But it just looked like a beaker full of water.

"I call it H2Info," she said. "Scientists have talked about the idea of storing information in liquid form for years. But I imagined going a step further. What if, instead of just storing information as a liquid and then putting the liquid in a machine that could read it like a disk, you cut out the middle step? What if you could ingest the liquid and have the information transferred directly to your mind?" She shook the beaker slightly. "There are millions of nanomachines in here . . . tiny drones that can interpret the information coded into the water molecules and create new neural pathways . . . literally writing information into the brain."

"Wow," Fisher said. "What's in this one?"

"'Baa Baa Black Sheep' in Russian," she said, looking a little sheepish. "I needed something simple for this first test. I'm going to call a physicist friend in Saint Petersburg and see how I do. Wish me luck!" With that, she tossed back the liquid and walked upstairs, already humming the rhyme.

"I'd better put this little guy back in his tank and get back to work," Mr. Bas said, patting Paul on the head and scooping him into his arms before heading up himself.

"They don't suspect a thing," Fisher said, smiling at his brother as FP hopped around their feet. "We'll have to keep a low profile tomorrow, but since the park is so big and there are only two of us—"

A chime sounded at a control panel in the hall. Somebody was at the gate. Alex quickly tapped the button to manually mist-ify the Liquid Door without bothering to ask the house who it was.

"Uh, yeah," Alex said, "about that . . . " He opened the door.

Amanda Cantrell stood on the step, black hair shimmering, glasses gleaming in the sun.

"Hey," she said.

"Hey," Alex replied, glancing nervously over his shoulder at Fisher.

She glanced over her own shoulder, as if worried someone had followed her. "You got it?" she said, dropping her voice to a whisper.

"I got it," Alex said.

"It?" Fisher said. "What is 'it'?" He crossed his arms.

Alex reached into his backpack and pulled out a small plastic card.

"Wait a minute, wait a minute," Fisher said, rushing forward and snatching it from Alex's hand. "Is that one of our parents' Loopity Land passes? We can't steal them before *they* need them or they'll find out, that's the whole reason I made the pickpocket drone! Besides, *we* were going to use the passes."

Alex gave Fisher a very large, very fake smile, reached into his backpack again, and pulled out a whole sheaf of the specially encrypted entrance cards. Amanda quickly tucked them into her own bag.

"I didn't steal them," Alex said. "Or, well, I did steal one, briefly. I figured out how to duplicate them. With CURTIS's help."

Fisher's eye started to twitch, and he fought down a surge of irritation. How could Alex have plotted with Amanda behind Fisher's back when Fisher had trusted him to plot with Fisher behind their parents' backs!

"Let me get this straight," Fisher said in a harsh whisper. "You conspired with my artificial intelligence behind my back to make counterfeit tickets. You're going to flood the park with kids, and people will find out, and then—"

"I made one for Veronica, too," Alex interjected.

At the mention of Veronica Greenwich, Fisher's objections got into a pileup somewhere between his soft palate and his teeth, realized they weren't needed anymore, and retreated back down his throat.

" . . . Okay," Fisher said after a minute. His cheeks felt like he had Bunsen burners under them. Amanda smirked.

"Glad that's settled," Alex said. "Don't worry, Fisher. It's a big park, and we'll make sure the kids keep a low profile. Besides, I engineered the passes to self-destruct after use so they can't be traced back to us. All our friends agreed that if they get caught by security, they'll claim to have snuck in."

"Good thinking," Fisher said, ignoring the anxiety that resurged after Alex said *all our friends* and wondering if it was sad that the mere thought of his dream girl could defeat him so easily. He could take on evil robots, evil clones, and evil mad scientists, but the thought of one single, beautiful girl stopped Fisher's brain right in its tracks.

Sharing the brand-new Loopity Land with Veronica wasn't a chance Fisher could ever have passed up—Alex knew him too well. Even with things so good between Veronica and him, Fisher was still just beginning to figure out how to act around her and what made her happy. It wasn't as straightforward as relativity or advanced particle physics. Loopity Land was a risk, but one well worth taking. Besides, how wrong could things possibly go?

≋ CHAPTER 2 ≋

The problem with good ideas is that most people don't
have them.   —Dr. X, Prison Diary

Fisher pressed himself up against the metal gates of the
brand-new, one-of-a-kind Loopity Land. With the cau-
tiousness of a secret agent on a life-or-death mission,
Fisher scanned the entrance to the most high-tech amusement park in the world. He hoped Alex's fabricated tickets
would pass the test.

Joining Fisher and Alex on their mission were FP,
Amanda, Veronica, and three other seventh graders:
Trevor Weiss, with one of his vintage pencil cases sticking from his pants pocket, Erin "Mac" McLemore, a tall
girl who was one of Amanda's wrestling teammates, and
Warren Deveraux, whose constant twitching and bounc-
ing was the only thing that kept him awake.

"Just look at this place," said Erin, looking past the tall
gates at the rides that towered into the air. "Your folks
really built it?"

"Well, they designed it," Alex said, opening a canvas
tote bag next to FP and using a carrot stick to lure the
little pig inside. Alex scooped the now-wriggling bag onto

his shoulder. "I don't think putting a hammer or a drill in either of their hands would be a good idea."

"You sure you're all right carrying FP?" Fisher said.

"Sure," Alex said with a small wink. "We're pals now. Right, boy?" Alex patted the side of the bag. A faint snort sounded in reply.

"Oh man oh man oh man!" said Warren, almost tap-dancing as he bobbed. "I don't know what ride to try first. Maybe bumper cars. Are there bumper cars? If there aren't maybe there are bumper bikes or bumper unicycles or—"

"Hold it, hold it," Fisher said, putting a hand on Warren's shoulder. "We're not supposed to be here at all. Remember that. As far as our parents know, the eight of us are going to the movies." Fisher didn't add that they'd been so happy to hear he was actually socializing with other humans, they hadn't bothered to ask which movie or when. "We've got to be careful, so follow my lead once we're inside, okay? *Okay*?"

Warren, who had started to doze off as soon as Fisher started talking, snapped back to attention and nodded rapidly. Amanda and Trevor gave nods as well.

Fisher turned back to the gate. His parents and people with *real* invitations were already inside the park, touring the place, examining the rides, and doing whatever else they planned to do. Fisher hadn't seen any other

Plans for
PICKPOCKET DRONE

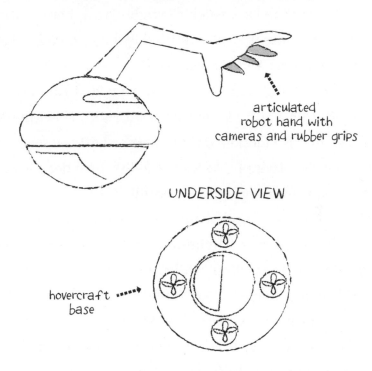

articulated
robot hand with
cameras and rubber grips

UNDERSIDE VIEW

hovercraft
base

kids: just the Bases' fellow scientists and technicians. Fisher was surprised just how many there were—the guests numbered in the hundreds at least. Either his parents were being extremely careful with these tests, or the rides were more complicated than he'd thought.

Still, given the size of the place, if the seventh graders were careful, they should be able to enjoy the rides undetected.

The entrance to the park was an elaborate main gate

with an archway, topped with LOOPITY LAND in huge, glowing, plastic letters across it, but the area under the arch turned out to be a thick Plexiglas wall. Four sliding doors were set into it, each guarded by large men in black fatigues, helmets, and tactical vests.

"I'll take point," said Alex. Fisher nodded him ahead. Alex moved forward, looking left and right, checking for their parents. He motioned them forward after a moment. Fisher led the others up to the gate, taking a deep breath as the mountainous guards examined them.

"Passes please," said a massive, gruff-throated man from behind mirrored aviators. Fisher fanned all the passes out for inspection, glancing sideways at Alex as the helmeted behemoth took them in a hand that looked like it could turn a baseball to powder.

Fisher's neck was starting to sweat. The guard's scanner was taking an awfully long time to process the passes. Fisher mentally cursed himself for blindly trusting Alex. These guards didn't look like the type of security that would send the kids away with a stern word and a finger waggle if they caught you.

Just when Fisher wondered if there was a little cement room with a single lightbulb in his near future, the scanner gave a little beep.

"Go ahead," the man said finally, handing the passes back. "Enjoy your visit to Loopity Land." His tone of voice suggested he'd been meaning to look up what "enjoy" meant but hadn't gotten around to it.

Fisher let out a long-held breath as he stepped forward and the transparent door serving as the park's high-tech gate slid to the side with the *fissshk* of brand-new, polished Plexiglas. One by one, the others followed him through. Fisher felt the passes getting warm in his hands, and he dropped them as they flared up and turned to ash.

"Whoa!" Erin said, taking a step back. "You really mean business, huh?"

"Our parents mean business," said Fisher, dusting the soot from his hands.

"All right, is everyone ready to have a good time?" Alex asked, sliding a pair of silver sunglasses down over his eyes. Everyone smiled and nodded. Alex unslung the tote bag from his shoulder and let FP hop out. Veronica beamed at Fisher, who, before his natural terror instinct could stop him, boldly reached out and took her hand.

"Okay then," Alex went on, unbuttoning the cuffs of his slick blue dress shirt and rolling his sleeves. "There's only two rules. First, we meet at the M3 coaster in the middle of the park in half an hour. Second, if anyone sees our parents, move immediately in the *other* direction. Because our parents typically go for several months at a time in between seeing the sun and most of you haven't met them, I've distributed pictures to your cell phones.

Other than that, all I ask . . . "—he paused dramatically and looked over his shades—"is that you take this place for all it's worth."

Amanda rolled her eyes slightly behind her glasses, but smiled in spite of it, and they were off. Erin, Trevor, and Warren immediately went in search of bumper cars, while Amanda hauled Alex off in another direction. Fisher smiled up at Veronica. As far as he was concerned, nothing they might do today, rides, games, whatever the park might throw at them, would be able to top the sheer excitement and joy he felt simply holding Veronica's hand. They could be walking through an empty warehouse and the thrill would be no less. FP trotted between Veronica and Fisher, munching on the discarded snack remains that occasionally dotted the path.

As they began moving through the park, Fisher was taken a little aback by the immensity of Loopity Land. And how *precisely* everything was laid out. The walkways all followed exact curves and angles, spreading in an intricate, and totally symmetrical, pattern. The grass was purple; whether it was a natural purple grass or had been dyed, Fisher couldn't tell. But it was remarkable, as were the shrubs and trees that decorated the walkways, which were oddly shaped and colored themselves. It was a mad scientist's dreamland. At perfectly even intervals, the spires and towers of the larger rides dominated the landscape, with smaller booths and attractions filling in the terrain at exact spots.

Some of the rides were truly gigantic. A long-drop free fall booth slowly climbed its way up a ten-story tower before plummeting back to Earth, making a gentle stop just before it threatened to plunge down through the Earth's crust. Another ride, modeled after the solar system, stretched steel arms out far over their heads and cut through the air with a rush. FP squeaked joyfully when they passed a carousel that was entirely made up of winged pigs.

It was almost as if the park was a machine, some kind of vast, extremely complicated device engineered to fulfill a specific purpose. Maybe it was the size of the rides, maybe it was the exacting angles and the perfect geometry, but it seemed somehow *unearthly.*

"Have you noticed all the security, Fisher?" Veronica said, still holding Fisher's hand and pointing subtly through the smiling crowds to the guards patrolling the main fence, which was made of thick steel cabling strung between heavy concrete pylons.

Fisher had been expecting fat men in short sleeve button-down shirts and Loopity Land baseball caps. But the guards here, like those outside the gates, looked like they belonged on a SWAT team. Helmets, armor, some carrying rifles. They moved briskly and purposefully, patrolling Loopity Land like it was filled with gold and former US presidents.

"It certainly seems excessive," Fisher said. "But my mom and dad are probably still on edge. After all, Dr. X did try to steal her top secret formula. Plus, there was the whole Three episode." But even as he said it, he wasn't convinced. "Maybe there's some new, secret technology built into the park that needs protecting?"

"Knowing your parents," Veronica said, "I wouldn't be surprised if there's a time-coaster that does a loop through 1973 in the middle." She stopped suddenly, squealing. "Fisher, look! Can we play?"

She was pointing to something that looked like the kind of typical target-shooting booth you'd see at any fair. Except in this case the target was a detailed scale model of a castle wall, and instead of water pistols or a BB gun sitting on the counter, there was a little catapult.

"Of course," Fisher said. "Come on." They stepped up to the polished steel booth. A short man in a blue jumpsuit with a black *LL* on the chest smiled at him from behind the counter.

"Morning!" said the worker. "If you'll take a moment to look behind me, you'll see various color-coded blocks in the castle wall. Blues are worth five points, greens are ten, and if you hit a red, it's an instant prize!" He gestured to the sides of the booth where a variety of plushy medieval-themed prizes were displayed. Then he tapped the foot-tall catapult. "The catapult has a number of force settings, marked on the side to the tenth of a Newton. The rack to the side holds ammunition assorted by precise weight."

Fisher rolled up the sleeves of his green turtleneck into uneven bunches as he'd seen Alex do. "Do you have scrap paper and a pencil?" he said.

The worker produced a pad of paper and a sharp pencil from under the counter. Fisher smiled at Veronica and began his calculations.

A few neat lines of equations later, Fisher selected a little metal ball of just the right weight, dropped it into the catapult's basket, set the lever, rotated the siege engine, and pressed the little release toggle. The ball cut a perfect arc through the air and knocked a red block out of the castle wall.

"And you win a prize!" the worker said. "Take your pick."

Fisher turned to Veronica and gestured toward the prizes. She grinned and pointed at a stuffed dragon, which the man picked out and handed to Fisher, who in turn presented it to Veronica.

"For my lady, the Duchess of Greenwich," Fisher said, bowing.

"Why, Sir Fisher, a gallant act indeed," Veronica replied

with a little giggle and a curtsy, reaching for the dragon.

A massive arm jutted in from nowhere and snatched the stuffed creature away before Veronica could take it. Fisher turned in confusion and horror to see Brody, leader of the Vikings, leering at him.

"Thanks, Basman," Brody said, clapping Fisher on the back so hard his glasses nearly flew off his face. "I always wanted one of these."

"What are you doing here?" Veronica half hissed. "How did you even get *in* here?"

"Why don't you ask your genius *boyfriend* to figure it out?" Brody said with a partially toothed smile. "I think I'll go share an ice cream with my new friend." With that, Brody lumbered away, clutching the dragon. *Veronica's* dragon.

"Let it go, Fisher," Veronica said quietly as Fisher nearly lunged after him.

But Fisher couldn't let it go. Wrath was flowing like magma through his veins. The world slowed down in Fisher's perception. He saw Brody's path as a series of numbers—velocity and distance, trajectory and destination. Without hesitation, he grabbed another metal ball, spun the catapult to face out, loaded, and fired.

Brody was guffawing to himself when the tiny projectile smacked the back of his head. He stumbled, almost fell, and turned. Fisher could see the mindless rage in his eyes. Which was really the only kind of rage Brody experienced.

"Time to go," Fisher said, picking up FP in one hand and grabbing Veronica's hand with the other. They took off down a path toward the middle of the park. Brody was out of sight behind them by the time they reached an open spot where three paths crossed.

They almost crashed into Alex and Amanda, running from one direction, and Trevor, Erin, and Warren, running from another.

"Brody's here!" Fisher said.

"So's Willard!" said Alex.

"And Leroy," said Trevor.

"Come on," Alex said, "let's find somewhere to hide."

"Um . . . " Trevor said, craning his neck and pointing. "What about there?"

Fisher looked up. There it was: the Mega Mars Madness Coaster. He could definitely see the madness part. The M3 ride formed a giant circle, and the track went around and around and around so many times it was wonderfully nauseating just looking at it. The coaster was a giant, tightly woven coil. There weren't any sudden changes in direction or smaller loops. The thrill came from raw speed. If Fisher remembered the diagrams correctly, the coaster went really, *really* fast.

It was perfect. The group headed straight for the M3.

As they got closer, the coaster's size became even more apparent, and Fisher felt almost intimidated in its shadow, like a barbarian merchant taking his first look at the Coliseum in Rome.

But their excitement was short-lived. When the seventh graders reached M3's entrance they saw why there was no line: A white banner was strung above the waiting cars with big black letters spelling out **CLOSED—M3 STILL IN PROGRESS.**

Now, scrutinizing the tracks and supports, Fisher could see that middle of the coaster held a broad circle of perfectly mowed grass. It was at least two hundred feet wide. He couldn't figure out what the field was for. It looked as though something else was supposed to be there—something that hadn't been constructed yet.

"Fisher," Alex whispered harshly, just as Trevor let out a squeak of fear.

"Here they come . . . " Amanda said.

Fisher turned and saw the Vikings. The trio of almost perfectly cubic beings thudded along the path, their swollen feet hitting the pavement like wet sandbags, their dull, half-lidded eyes probing weakly for any sign of prey.

Brody, the leader, his forehead sloped like a steamroller, clenched and unclenched fists the size of flowerpots. Willard, the stammerer, whose left eye twitched with the weak, random pulses of his laboring brain. Leroy, the language killer, moved like a pile of laundry falling down a staircase.

"We've handled them before," Veronica said coolly. "We can do it again."

"Yeah," Fisher said, thinking again of the dragon, which Brody had apparently stolen only to ditch somewhere, probably in the nearest trash can. "Let's remind them what happens when you mess with the Bas boys."

"Wait." Alex shook his head. "We're supposed to be keeping a low profile, remember? I don't think feuding with the Vikings counts."

Fisher stared at his brother. For once, Alex was being the rational one. "You're right," he admitted. "Come on. There's room in the cars." He pointed to the coaster's open seats. "If we duck, we'll be okay. And we can plot our revenge some other time."

As the Vikings trudged closer, Fisher and his friends sprinted to the cars and hopped in, ducking below the high sides to keep from view. Warren promptly fell asleep, and Trevor had to elbow him when he began snoring.

"Everyone here?" Fisher whispered. A chorus of quiet "yeses" and "yeps" answered.

"Where's FP?" whispered Veronica next to him.

"Oh, no . . . " Fisher sighed, sticking his head up. FP

was still happily wandering around where they'd left him. "FP!" he said as loudly as he dared. "Come over here, boy!" he beckoned.

FP noticed him, started wagging his curly tail cheerfully, backed up several paces, dashed forward, and took off, spreading his little leg-wings.

"Fisher . . . " Alex warned. Fisher saw it. FP's trajectory, as usual, was all wrong. He hurdled over them, and straight into the open window of the locked control room.

There was a *beep*. Followed by an ominous *click*.

Before anyone could react, the coaster started forward with a jerky lurch. It rapidly picked up speed, racing to ascend the first loop. By the time they realized what was happening, it was too late to get out.

"Everyone into the seats!" shouted Amanda, her voice carried away by the wind. "Lock your harnesses!" Fisher helped lower Veronica's safety harness into place and then hastily locked his own, and not a moment too soon. The M3's acceleration picked up, and up and up, with no telling when it would stop.

A single terrified thought gripped Fisher's mind, and, clearly, everyone else's: just how unfinished *was* this roller coaster?

≋ CHAPTER 3 ≋

When all else fails, whatever you have left will also probably fail. —Three, Cell Wall Writings

Fisher's eyes began to water as M3 careened around the circular track. The force of acceleration crushed Fisher into the padded seat. That "incomplete" sign had been put there for a reason: the M3 wasn't ready yet. Any moment, they could hit a spot of missing track they hadn't seen, and go hurtling through the air like the stone Fisher had catapulted at the castle wall. And they were moving so fast, they probably wouldn't even know it until they hit the ground hard enough to set off the San Andreas Fault.

The M3 finished its first full circle and tore into the second with blinding speed as Fisher's vision blurred into a continuous, full-spectrum blob. It was like someone had dropped a kaleidoscopic fishbowl over his head. The rushing of the wind, the screeching of the tracks, and the screams of the other kids all blended into a smoothie of terror.

The M3 barreled into its second loop. The Vikings must have seen the coaster moving by now. Would they think to try and stop it? Probably not, since it would require that they think, period. Fisher didn't like the idea of having his life saved by the Vikings, but having his life *not* be saved would definitely be worse.

Fisher tried to reach out and put his hand on Veronica's, but his arm was pinned in place by the velocity of M3. He felt like his joints were about to pop out of place.

Fisher's cheeks flared out like a bulldog caught in a high-speed car chase from the wind. He managed to turn and see if Veronica was all right. Veronica's brilliant golden hair looked like it was being blown dry by a helicopter, but she looked unharmed. He couldn't see the rest of his friends, but their intermittent yelps and shouts reassured Fisher that they were at least still pinned to their seats.

An abrupt shift pushed Fisher forward against his harness—they were slowing down! As the trees zipped by, Fisher realized that they were descending.

Mercifully, the ride finally came to an end, new brakes shrieking, an elephant sitting on Fisher's chest as the last of the coaster's momentum was used up. It took Fisher a few seconds to recover his senses and realize the cars had stopped moving. With shaking hands he unlatched his harness and pushed it up away from him. He'd barely shrugged it off when Veronica plunged into his arms, and his already erratic pulse shot right back up into the red.

"I thought we were going to crash," she said, leaning into him. "Are you okay?"

"Yes," he said, "I think . . . I hope I'm still alive."

She pulled away slightly, and suddenly her face was four inches from his. A newly activated part of Fisher's mind started tap-dancing around like its socks had been stuffed with gravel and ghost peppers.

You've seen this moment in movies a million billion times, it said. *You know what happens now!*

Fisher wasn't sure whether to trust this part of his brain.

What do you mean you're not sure?? I thought you'd learned not to run and hide from human contact by now! Come on, Fisher. You know what to do.

Fisher started to lean toward Veronica. A little wisp of a smile flickered across her face.

He was going to do it. . . . He was going to kiss her. . . .

"WAHHHH!" Alex shouted at the top of his lungs, rattling them both out of the moment. Alex was pointing up at the sky. A massive fiery object was plunging directly toward them.

Amanda screamed, "GO!"

Then the top of the Mega Mars Madness coaster exploded. Fisher's hearing was instantly blown out. A dull ringing echoed in his ears as he scrambled out of the car and away from the coaster. He escaped not a moment too soon—his hand tight around Veronica's as he pulled her away from the fiery mass barreling toward their heads. Alex, Amanda, and the others ran alongside them. The Earth shook like a struck bell, and Fisher was thrown from his feet and swallowed by a cloud of dust.

Everything went black.

For a moment, Fisher thought he must be dead. Then he realized if he were dead he wouldn't have the capacity to reflect on it. He sat up, groaning a little, trying to blink the grit from his eyes. His hearing was just starting to come back and he heard an alarm begin to blare.

They had been encircled by a wall of tangled, shredded steel and tortured, burning plastic. Half the remains of the M3 formed a barrier encircling the coaster park. The other half had been reduced to a heap the size of an office building that the kids had barely avoided being buried under. Trevor and Erin were lying on the ground, petrified but miraculously uninjured. Alex was helping Amanda to her feet. She winced as though she'd sprained her ankle. From the sound of commotion outside the wall of debris, a crowd was running in their direction, hopefully with plenty of emergency equipment.

Only then did Fisher realize that Veronica's hand was no longer in his.

"Alex!" he shouted. Panic burned through his veins

like fire. "Veronica!" It was the only thing he could say. Luckily, Alex understood.

Fisher dashed back into the debris in a panic, hurling everything he could lift out of the way. Amanda nodded to Alex that she was okay, and he ran to help, along with Erin. The guards were setting up barriers, forming a perimeter around the wreck and talking hurriedly into their radios.

"Did you see what happened to her?" yelled Alex. To Fisher, whose hearing was still scrambled, it sounded as if Alex was whispering through four layers of Styrofoam.

"No," Fisher said desperately. "I had her hand as we were running away, but I lost her when we got knocked over."

"We can't find Warren, either," Alex said as he started hefting and heaving through the rubble alongside Fisher.

With every lifted-away piece that didn't reveal Veronica, Fisher's frantic pace increased. He almost tossed a piece of scrapped plastic right into Alex's head, forcing his clone to duck. Fisher yelled an apology and kept digging.

He turned at the muffled sound of a familiar squeal-snort.

FP bounded out of the wreckage, looking heroic—winged hooves prancing. He darted past Fisher and Alex and hopped from one piece of debris to another, putting his snout to each. Then he stopped and let out a piercing squeal, shaking his curly tail like a maraca.

"Veronica!?" Fisher's heart was in his chest. If anything had happened to her, he would never forgive himself.

Fisher and Alex shoved until Fisher's arms burned with overstrain, and they just managed to shift a massive support strut out of the way. Underneath it was Veronica. The huge C-shaped beam that landed over her had actually shielded her from other debris. She squirmed free, her hair and clothing matted in dust. She wrapped her arms around Fisher until his lungs barely worked, ashes from the explosion puffing off of her like a coating of flour.

"Oof . . . youf ofkay?" Fisher's voice was muffled by her shoulder.

"I'm okay," she said. "I'm okay. Is everyone else all right?"

"FP found Warren!" Alex shouted. "He's fine! Asleep, actually."

Fisher kicked something with his heel as he stepped back from Veronica. He looked down to see a twisted, bent steel tube. It took a moment for him to realize it was a safety harness. He felt nauseous. They could have *died*. They almost *had* died.

Fisher led Veronica back to the group. The others were still picking themselves up and brushing themselves off.

Erin, who always kept a small first-aid kit on her, had just finished taping up Amanda's ankle. Amanda tested it and grimaced, but nodded.

"It's not bad," she said. "I can walk okay."

It wasn't until that moment that Fisher remembered Brody, Willard, and Leroy.

"Hang on," he said with what little breath he could draw. "What about the Vikings? They were near the coaster when it started. Are we sure they got away in time?"

"I saw them walking away as we got going," Erin said. "Unless they doubled back they are probably fine."

Fisher could hear dozens of voices outside the barrier of wreckage the explosion had ringed them with. Underneath them was a grumbling engine and heavy metallic clangs. It sounded like a bulldozer or a backhoe was clearing a path.

"Sounds like we'll be out of here soon," Alex said, putting his arm around Amanda's shoulders.

"So . . . Did all of you see that?" Veronica said, tilting her head upward.

"Of course we saw it," grumbled Amanda. "How do you not see a fifty-foot meteor pointed right at your head?"

"It wasn't a meteor," Veronica said. "It was a ship."

Everyone stared at her like she'd sprouted a parrot beak.

"Veronica," Amanda said, moving toward her and speaking very slowly, "are you sure you weren't hurt?

Did you bump your head? Maybe someone should take a look." She lifted a hand toward her head. Veronica brushed it away.

"I'm not hallucinating," she said impatiently. "I'm fine. I know what I saw." She turned to Fisher. "You believe me, don't you?"

Fisher opened his mouth and closed it again, feeling a little bit like a fish trying to swallow an apple.

Alex yanked Fisher aside and spoke quietly. "Fisher, an object that size falling from space should've turned this whole park into talcum powder. You know that."

"Yeah," Fisher muttered back, pretending he hadn't noticed that Veronica was now glaring at him. "It would have to have been moving pretty slowly to just wreck the coaster. But a *ship*?"

"Uh, everybody?" said Erin, pointing to the wreckage. "What is *that*?"

Seeping from between the shattered remains of the M3 coaster was a viscous green fluid that glowed faintly. It flowed over obstacles and even *up* them, defying gravity—almost as if it were alive. More and more of it pooled in the grass as Fisher and the others backed away.

Soon, it had formed a circular pool the size of the Wompalog basketball court. The faint green glow seemed to pulse calmly, like a very slow heartbeat. Then it started to move again.

Nobody could speak. Not even Alex could think of anything clever to say.

A narrow tendril rose out of the pool and slowly extended toward the kids, who were rooted to the spot like a row of flowers. Very confused, scared flowers. The tendril paused when it reached Amanda and Veronica, and its end widened into something like a satellite dish. It stayed in place for a few seconds before the whole extrusion zipped back into the puddle.

The fluid then divided into thirteen forms that rose and stretched upward. As the forms solidified, they took on oddly familiar shapes; torsos, arms, legs, then heads. Colors and textures appeared next, becoming skin, hair, even clothing. Fisher was too flabbergasted to even have a sense of how long the whole process took, but it couldn't have been more than a minute.

Where there had once been a small pond of luminescent green gloop, there were now thirteen very attractive and fashionable-looking teenage girls.

Veronica crossed her arms and shot Fisher a dirty look. "See? I *told* you it was a ship."

≋ CHAPTER 4 ≋

First Contact with aliens is a delicate process. You want to present humanity as a gentle, kind, and enlightened people. You can always tell them the truth later.

—Vic Daring, Issue #23

Here it was. Extraterrestrial life. *Aliens.* Fisher had spent every single day of his life trying to imagine what this exact moment might be like for humanity.

He hadn't, however, imagined that he, Fisher Bas, would be the first human to *meet* the alien race—especially not at twelve years old.

Nor had he anticipated their appearance. These beings were obviously not human. Or even carbon-based. But they looked exactly like teenage girls. *Gorgeous* ones. Veronica was still the most beautiful girl Fisher had ever seen, but staring at a thirteen-way tie for second place was dizzying. The aliens looked like a team of superheroines selected from all over the planet. They were all ethnicities, different heights and appearances, but all looked the same age, and all radiated beauty.

"Uh . . . " Fisher said. He realized Alex was making the same sound. It was the same noise that rattles out of an old laptop when it's trying to analyze particle accelerator data. Fisher's brain was in overdrive.

The "girls" turned to look at the humans. Their eyes clicked to Fisher's, and then to Alex's, and then back. Then, with a signal that was invisible to Fisher, the girls began to glow. Each one became . . . blurry. Almost as if they were vibrating at extremely high frequency. The blurriness increased, making them look like doubles.

After a moment it became clear that doubling was *exactly* what they were doing. Twin forms grew farther apart until, with a final snap into clarity, each girl became a pair of identical twins, right down to their clothing and the way their hair fell.

The identical two girls closest to Fisher and Alex stepped forward. They were pale, with ice-blonde hair. Electric green eyes held Fisher's attention in a vise grip.

"Hello," one said in a voice that was like soft violin music played in front of a gentle waterfall. "We've been studying your species from space for many years. We were only waiting for a signal from you to make contact."

"Signal?" Fisher squeaked out.

"We're so happy to meet the official Earth representatives!" the other said with a glowing smile that made Fisher feel like stammering even though he wasn't talking. "We hope that our arrival wasn't inconvenient."

"No, no, no, not at all," Fisher said, marveling at how

easy it was to serve as the ambassador for Earth's first encounter with an alien species. He could feel the Nobel Prize slipping into his hands already. He blinked to clear his mind. The fact that the aliens looked like pretty girls was distracting him from the fact that they were *aliens*. Nobody in recorded history had ever even found proof of extraterrestrial beings, let alone spoken to one face-to-face. Out of nowhere, Fisher and his friends were standing directly in the middle of one of the biggest moments in history.

"We're *fine*," Amanda said, hopping on her stronger ankle to get a better look at the girls. "No thanks to you."

"Where did you come from?" Trevor asked in an awed whisper.

"We're from a star system approximately five hundred Earth light-years from yours," said the first twin. "We are called . . . " The two girls made a series of sounds that fell somewhere between whale song and a jackhammer hitting a submarine, accompanied by flashes of light from their eyes.

"Um . . . " Fisher and Alex said, exchanging a look. Fisher cleared his throat. "Can you repeat that?"

"We're aware that your physiology is incapable of reproducing our name," said the second girl, "even though humans can make lots of wonderful sounds." She flashed Fisher another warm grin. Even Veronica didn't smile at him this much. "Because of that, you may decide upon a human name for our species that you are more comfortable saying."

"What about the Landing Impaired?" Amanda said.

"Or the Altitude Recalibration?" Veronica added.

"Veronica," Fisher whispered. "Don't be—" But when she turned to glare at him, he swallowed back the word *rude.*

"Well, they're all twins," said Erin after a few seconds of uncomfortable silence. "Twins from space. That reminds me of the astronomy unit in my science class. We could call them the Gemini."

"Yes, yes," Fisher said quickly before Amanda and Veronica could say anything more. "The Gemini. Perfect."

"Yeah," Alex said. "Perfect . . . "

Amanda cleared her throat. Actually it sounded more like she was clearing her entire thoracic cavity.

"We, uh," Alex said, glancing nervously at Amanda, "should give you Earth names individually, too."

"Fine," said Amanda, stepping up to Alex, putting her arm through his with pointed force, and giving the two Gemini who'd been speaking an iron-tipped glare. "It'll be tough to remember a lot of complicated names. There are twenty-six of you. So we'll name you alphabetically. Anna and Bee," she said, pointing to the speakers.

She proceeded with the rest of them, pointing and naming, and if any of the other kids disagreed with her they definitely knew better than to go up against the wrestling captain. Fisher tapped a button in his sleeve, switching on a hidden digital recorder to get the names down, hoping it hadn't been damaged during the crash.

"Yang and Zoe," Amanda finished.

The second Gemini, Bee, nodded in approval. "That's perfect."

"Well, good," said Fisher. "Great, in fact! As, um, Earth representative, I . . . uh-oh."

A mound of rubble and dirt clods was pushed apart from inside, and a trio of familiar faces appeared with perfectly bad timing.

The Vikings. So they'd come back after all, just in time to be caught by the blast.

"Hey!" shouted Brody, looking as angry and stupid as usual. They stormed forward at Fisher.

But they stopped cold when they saw the Gemini. The Vikings looked at each other, unsure of how to act in the presence of so much beauty, their faces flushing.

Brody was the first to snap out of it. "We got business with you," he said, pointing at Fisher with a broad stub of a finger.

"Y-yeah," Willard said, taking a step forward. "P-punching b-business."

Ingrid and Jeanne (Gemini girls nine and ten) neatly intercepted them.

LIST OF GEMINI NAMES
and brief descriptions***

1. Anna
2. Bee
very blonde, green eyes
leaders, gorgeous

3. Claire
4. Deb
very tall, wow so pretty

5. Ellie
6. Fae
red hair, flickering a lot
might explode? stunning

7. Gloria
8. Helen
intensely beautiful,
brunettes

9. Ingrid
10. Jeanne
exquisite, definitley exploded

11. Kat
12. Leah
short hair, breathtaking

13. Mae
14. Nina
curly hair, extremely pretty

15. Ophelia
16. Phoebe
bright blue eyes,
stunningly beautiful

17. Quinn
18. Renée
extremely tall, so so pretty

19. Sandy
20. Tina
glasses, devastatingly
gorgeous, you get the idea

21. Ulyana
22. Vera
jet black hair, surprise:
magnificently stunning

23. Wendy
24. Xena
just wow

25. Yang
26. Zoe
super gorgeous

***none are as
pretty as Veronica

"Excuse us," said Ingrid sweetly. "We're in conversation with the ambassadors. You're interrupting us."

"This isn't your business," said Brody. But he sounded nervous. "You tell 'em, Willard."

Willard gulped a little and puffed himself up. "Yeah. It isn't your business. So . . . just . . . g-get out of our way. Why don't you just . . . go do c-cartwheels??"

"Yeah," said Leroy. "You look like a bunch of dumb, squawking, uh, pairs o' cleats."

"Parakeets," corrected Brody, smacking his forehead.

Ingrid and Jeanne frowned deeply. Then they started to glow. Fisher heard a faint hissing sound. The hiss grew into a harsh crackle, like a big log in a fireplace or very violent popcorn. *BOOM.*

Fisher blinked and staggered backward as another blast nearly knocked him off his feet. Had the Gemini shot the Vikings with some kind of high-energy particle beam?

When his vision cleared, he saw the Vikings were flat on the ground, marked with cuts, bruises, and burns. One of Brody's eyes was swollen shut and Willard was holding one arm like it was broken. On the spot where Ingrid and Jeanne had been standing there was now little more than a scorch mark and a small puddle of green fluid.

Two Gemini had *exploded.* Oddly, the other twenty-four girls didn't really seem to care.

Fisher and Alex jumped at a second earsplitting noise.

But it wasn't the Gemini this time. It was the crash of a bulldozer finally breaking through the debris of the M3. That crash was followed by the sound of heavy boots as the guards raced through the gap the dozer had created.

"Step away from the aliens!" the team leader said, forming a semicircle behind the kids.

Fisher spent a second wondering how the guards knew the Gemini were aliens. Maybe the people farther away had seen the ship coming. But Fisher didn't have long to wonder. He knew things were about to go from bad to worse. His heart sped back up to panic mode. Everything had been going so well until the Vikings had shown up.

Now they were on the verge of interstellar war.

≋ CHAPTER 5 ≋

The human species is its own natural predator, and is quite good at it.
                                    —Early Gemini notes on Earth

The Gemini started glowing. They reminded Fisher of deep-sea bioluminescent fish, sending out an eerie red light from just beneath their skin. The heavy brow of the security team's leader twitched as he eyed the girls, his weapon hovering at the ready in his thick, blue-veined hands.

"Wait! Wait!" Fisher said, running up to the leader of the guards. "Please don't agitate them. They . . . they don't take it well."

"We saw the explosion," the guard said coolly, his eyes not moving from the aliens for even an instant. "I'd say how they've acted so far gives us every reason to believe they're hostile."

The scientists had poured in through the breach and were gathering in a loose half circle behind the guards, chattering among themselves and calibrating various handheld instruments. Still, Fisher didn't see his parents. Where *were* they?

One of the guards grabbed Fisher by the arm; another one grabbed Alex. The Gemini glow became more intense, along with the crackle sound. The area was bathed in their light, which strobed slowly and menacingly.

"Stop!" Fisher shouted. He managed to shake free of the huge man's grasp. "They're not hostile. They think you're trying to hurt us. They're trying to protect us."

"Fisher," Veronica whispered harshly. She didn't look exceptionally pleased that Fisher was defending extraterrestrial beings whose chief method of debate seemed to be self-detonation.

"Nobody was badly hurt in the explosion," Alex said, fighting his way out of the other guard's grip. "Well . . . no humans, at least." He looked again at the sooty spot that had been Ingrid and Jeanne. "The aliens have a . . . some kind of natural defense mechanism. They thought we were in trouble."

Amanda glared at him.

The guards paused, exchanging bewildered glances, clearly unsure how to proceed.

"Stand down, Sergeant," said a calm, familiar voice. The sergeant lowered his weapon and stepped back, gesturing for his men to do the same, as Fisher's parents stepped forward between them.

In that moment, Fisher was reminded that his mom and dad weren't just his mom and dad. They were titans of the scientific community. Helen Bas wore her long white lab coat like a knight's armor. Fisher could practically *see* Walter Bas's incredible mind humming along at speeds most people couldn't imagine. The rest of the scientists treated them like nobility.

"Mom!" said Alex and Fisher. Fisher was incredibly relieved to see that his parents were here, and all right. At the same time, he felt a pinch of dread: they'd been busted, pure and simple. He raced to come up with an excuse. Maybe he could say he rushed here to warn them of something. A sudden outbreak of reactivated Fisher-bots? The home lab was on fire? Paul had accidentally hugged the lever that released Mr. Bas's semi-intelligent plastic-eating ants into the wild?

But Mrs. Bas looked right past Alex and Fisher and beamed at the Gemini. As the guards backed off, the glow from the aliens dimmed and went out, and the crackling softened and finally went silent.

"This is a monumental event, boys," Mrs. Bas said in a trembling voice, putting a hand on each son's shoulders. "We've made first contact with a highly advanced extra-terrestrial species. You realize this moment will be taught in history classes for the rest of human civilization?"

Fisher exhaled. Of course, now that he thought about it, his act of minor trespassing had no significance next to the arrival of the Gemini. He just hoped the people who wrote those history books would spice up his dialogue a bit, and maybe give him more to say than "uh." He could already imagine the moment immortalized as a painted tableau: the Gemini, Fisher and Alex, the Bas parents; scientists and engineers with testing apparatuses buzzing; FP trying to nuzzle Warren awake.

Maybe, Fisher thought, the Vikings could be deleted from the scene. Currently, an EMT was treating them for their cuts and bruises. Fisher wondered whether the incident would finally teach them something about how approaching every situation by yelling at it can and will end badly. He wondered this for about two and a half seconds before remembering that the Vikings did not learn anything, ever.

"This has gone even better than we planned," Mrs. Bas went on.

"Planned?" squawked Alex and Fisher simultaneously.

Mrs. Bas smiled. "Astronomers have been tracking their ship for months. We suspect they've been in the solar system dozens of times, studying Earth, and us. However, they made no response to radio contact, so we designed something more *advanced.*"

Fisher's jaw dropped like a bowling ball through tissue paper.

"The M3," Alex breathed.

"Mega Mars Madness is just a cover name," said Mr.

Bas. "Its real name is the Magnetic Modulation Mechanism. The operation of the coaster creates a detectable ripple in Earth's magnetic field. We hoped it would be a sign to the ship that humanity was ready for interstellar contact. And it seems to have worked, if a little early. Today was a day to check and calibrate the systems. The big day was planned for next week."

So *that* was the signal that the Gemini had referred to.

Fisher gazed at his parents wonderingly. They'd been tracking an alien spacecraft for months and he'd had no idea. It must have been *unbearable* for them to keep from telling him.

His parents moved closer to the Gemini. The crowd unconsciously inched backward, as though worried about another explosion, but both Bas parents seemed entirely at ease.

"As the creators of the Magnetic Modulation Mechanism, the instrument that signaled our readiness to meet you, we'd like to formally welcome you to Earth," said Mrs. Bas to Anna and Bee. The two aliens turned to regard Fisher's parents with their vibrant green eyes, their expressions unreadable.

"Your engineering work is excellent," Bee said. Her voice was much flatter than it had been before, much more formal. "We regret that our landing telemetry had a slight inaccuracy and our ship caused damage."

"Damage" was a bit understated. What had been the Magnetic Modulation Mechanism looked like an abstract sculpture built by hurling the chopped-up pieces of a skyscraper out of planes. The perfect lawns and flawlessly polished rides surrounding it only emphasized how utterly demolished it was.

"It can be rebuilt," said Mrs. Bas. "What matters is that it worked." She paused and took Anna's hand in her own, giving it a motherly squeeze. Anna gave Mrs. Bas's hand a confused look. "Imagine what we can learn from one another," Mrs. Bas continued with a sincere smile.

"Yes," said Anna. "We wish to begin an exchange with your two diplomats promptly." She indicated Fisher and Alex.

Mr. and Mrs. Bas glanced at each other.

"Well," Mrs. Bas said, "*diplomats* may be a bit of an exaggeration."

"That is how we are prepared to work," Bee said. She and Anna crossed their arms. "Now that we have established contact, it would be an unnecessary hitch in the process if someone else took their place."

The Gemini looked stern.

"And this 'exchange.' An exchange of what, exactly?" Amanda said, raising an eyebrow.

"Knowledge," said Anna. "Information, history, culture.

We, of course, have years of data about you. But there are many questions that only a face-to-face discussion can properly answer."

"Of course," Veronica said, narrowing her eyes. "Face-to-face."

It was increasingly obvious to Fisher that neither Veronica nor Amanda were fans of the female extraterrestrials. Fisher had just stopped World War III from happening. He wasn't ready for it to begin again.

"That sounds great," Fisher said. "But"—he hurried on, in response to a glance from Veronica, to whom he was after all very loyal—"as much as I'd like to be the head of an interstellar conference, well . . . we have to go to school."

"School," said Bee instantly, tilting her head, a motion Anna copied exactly. "An institution of learning, the place where young human spawn are fashioned into adults. We can think of no better place to begin further study of your kind."

"I don't think that's wise," Mr. Bas said. "A school is a busy, unsterile, and unpredictable environment; it might be bewildering or even dangerous for you."

"I don't know," Fisher said, spirals of technological possibilities from contact with aliens twirling through his mind. "I think that could be a really good idea. They know about our culture, they speak our language, and they don't seem vulnerable to Earth bacteria. Letting them learn in our fully human environment might be the best idea!"

"As exciting as that sounds," Mr. Bas, "it still sounds risky. I think it would make more sense to study them more before we allow them to fully integrate into a situation like that."

Anna and Bee stared at Mr. Bas for an uncomfortably large number of seconds. They crossed their arms, exactly mirroring the pose of a teenage girl determined to go out on a Saturday night with her friends.

In perfect synch, all of the other Gemini crossed their arms, too.

"We will attend your school," Anna stated flatly.

"You don't understand," Mrs. Bas said, "for your own safety, that really isn't a good . . . er . . . " The Gemini had started to glow again. A sound like the beginning of a forest fire filled the air.

"We will attend your school," Bee said.

"Could . . . " Mrs. Bas said, "could we maybe discuss this in more detail elsewhe—"

"DOWN!" Amanda screamed, and dove, tackling Warren to the ground, as Ellie and Fae turned into a cloud of superheated vapor. In a second, their long limbs and radiant red hair turned into green explosive goop. Veronica ducked. Mr. and Mrs. Bas grabbed Fisher and Alex and pulled them both to the ground. Screams went up from the crowd.

FP barely managed to take wing and fly from the explosion. The edge of the fireball caught him and he sailed into Fisher's arms as Fisher sat up, and his right side was peppered with first-degree burns. His right ear was raw from the heat, and a distinct bacon scent wafted from him.

The guards dropped into firing crouches, weapons trained on the Gemini.

"Say the word," the sergeant said, closing one eye and aiming. The crackling got louder and louder.

"Everyone stop it! This instant," Mr. Bas said as he leapt back to his feet. He gave the Gemini a parental stare. "All right," he said, "if school is how you want to begin our diplomatic relationship, school it is."

Slowly, the crackling subsided, and the Gemini's glowing skin dimmed and went back to normal. The sergeant indicated that the guards should stand down.

Mr. and Mrs. Bas turned to the ten or twelve scientists clustered around the security barrier. After a minute of urgent, whispered conversation, Fisher's mom returned to face the Gemini.

"If you'd just come this way," Mrs. Bas said in the most lighthearted tone she could muster. She pointed to a futuristic-looking bus that was even now making its

THE GEMINI BUS

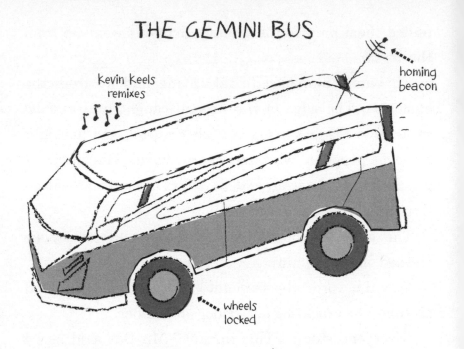

Kevin Keels
remixes

homing
beacon

wheels
locked

lumbering way through the park, "we have a vehicle pre-pared for you specially. This will be your temporary home. For the moment, you'll be stationed at a facility just next to our home. And, beginning Monday, you can all attend school . . . somehow."

The twenty-two Gemini filed onto the bus without another word, gliding through the crowd like a blowtorch through butter, escorted by a group of overeager scien-tists and members of the security SWAT team. As the last two Gemini boarded—Fisher couldn't remember their names—they paused, turned, smiled slyly at him with the exact same tilt to their heads, and gave a small wave.

Fisher found that he'd been holding his breath. As soon

as the bus began to pull away, he felt the beginnings of a throbbing headache. Could he have done anything to have made the interaction go better, or at least less explosive? History—or random chance, if he was being honest—had placed him at the forefront of human–Gemini relations.

And now the aliens wanted to go to Wompalog.

The prospect was terrifying. It was also the most exciting thing he'd ever imagined.

"Hey," Alex said to Fisher quietly, "you think maybe we should call Agent Mason?"

FBI Special Agent Syd Mason had originally been tasked with recovering any traces of Mrs. Bas's Accelerated Growth Hormone, which included Alex. After an unfortunate beginning Fisher, Alex, and Mason had eventually formed an alliance against Dr. X. Mason had even shown up at the last second to rescue them from the collapsing school after the final battle with Three. If there was ever a time to involve him, the surprise presence of alien life on Earth seemed appropriate.

"I doubt we need to," Fisher said. "He probably knew about the Gemini weeks ago like our parents. I bet he's here right now. He'll probably jump out from behind that tree any second," he went on, pointing to one of the few decorative elms around the coaster that hadn't been pulverized. Fisher and Alex stared at it expectantly. Agent Mason did not jump out from behind it.

"Hm," Fisher said. "Well, I can't imagine he's not involved in this somehow. If he doesn't turn up soon, we'll give him a call."

The Bas parents were still deep in conversation with their scientific colleagues. Fisher couldn't make out what they were saying, but from the expansiveness of their hand gestures, he knew they felt the same nervous excitement as he did about their new visitors.

FP, on the other hand, looked decidedly unenthusiastic. Fisher scooped up his squealing pig, examining the burn on FP's right ear. Fortunately, it looked superficial.

"Uh, Fisher?" Fisher felt a tap on his shoulder. He turned around and nearly dropped FP in surprise. Willard stood in front of him, his left arm in a sling and his face bandaged up. He was looking at the ground, almost as if he were embarrassed.

"I wanted to, uh . . . " He looked around quickly. Brody and Leroy were nowhere to be seen. " . . . apologize," he mumbled.

"Oh," Fisher said, and couldn't find another word in his head. This was almost as big a shock as the explosion of the roller coaster. Maybe almost getting blown across Loopity Land in several million smithereens had finally humbled Willard. Fisher cleared his throat. "I mean, that's okay. I'm just . . . relieved . . . you weren't seriously hurt." *Happy* would have been a bit of an overstatement.

"So, uh, how did you guys get in here, anyway?"

"We were t-tagging along with my d-dad," Willard replied, still staring at the space between his feet.

"How did your *dad* get in?" said Fisher, picturing a larger and even more gargoyle-shaped version of Willard. Maybe his dad worked for one of the scientists as a paperweight, or a standard for measuring density.

"H-he's on the team that's working with your parents," Willard said. "The Mission for Organized Retrieval of Objects from Nearby Space."

"MORONS?" Fisher said.

"Uh, y-yeah," Willard said. "They say they get that a lot from NASA. My dad's a p-propulsion research engineer."

Fisher felt like a pair of electric eels had just kissed his temples.

"Your father is a *rocket scientist*?" he said, not even trying to conceal his shock. Willard nodded, then made a second, awkward good-bye nod and hurried off. Fisher stared off after Willard, shaking his head. The surprises were piling high today.

"Hey, Fisher," said Veronica. FP wiggled in Fisher's arms and Veronica held up a tube of burn ointment she must have procured from an EMT. Gratefully, Fisher took it from her. For a moment, they stood in awkward silence as Fisher tried to figure out how Veronica must be feeling. After a minute, he remembered that he could, in fact, *ask* her. Some of the finer points of socializing were still solidifying in his mind.

"Are you all right?" he asked.

Veronica took the tube back from Fisher's hand and carefully applied the burn ointment onto FP's ear.

"I'm not sure," she said slowly, without looking up. "I mean, I understand this is a momentous event. I want to be happy. I want to welcome the Gemini with open arms. I just can't quite bring myself to trust them. I can't figure them out at all. What do they really want? Why are they so interested in Wompalog and not the UN or NASA?"

"I don't know," Fisher said, watching larger work crews move in to begin carting off the rubble and debris from the M3. "But the Gemini are far more advanced than we are. Given the kind of technology needed for long-range interstellar flight, I'd put them at least four or five hundred years ahead of us. Imagine what they've seen. What they must have discovered out there. And their technology! If they'd meant us harm, we'd all be dead by now."

"I hope so," said Veronica. "But not everything that glitters is gold. And if they don't even bat an eye when one of their own goes up in flames, I can't imagine they'd put much value on a human life."

Her normally brilliant eyes were dark, as if they'd been

smudged with ash. Her golden hair was frizzy from the explosion. And there was an urgency to her voice, a warning he struggled to understand.

"Are you saying that if I make a mistake, something bad could happen to me?" he asked.

"No," she said quietly. "I'm saying that if you make a mistake, something bad could happen to all of us."

≋ CHAPTER 6 ≋

I believe in taking on whatever the universe throws at you,
I just wasn't expecting the universe to take that challenge
so literally. —Alex Bas, Personal Notes

WEL . . . COME . . . TO . . . SCOOL

    WEL . . . COME . . . TO . . . SCOOL

"Hey, Fisher?" Veronica said, looking up at the huge scrolling LED sign Fisher had put above one of Wompalog's main trailers. "Think you might be missing something?"

"What?" Fisher said, marveling at it, his face aglow with a cheek-aching smile. "It all looks good to m—oh, no. No, no, no, no, no . . . " he repeated to himself as he ran to the control panel and frantically attempted to input the correct spelling of *school.*

To say that he was nervous would be an understatement. He was as jumpy as a cricket after five espressos.

WEL . . . COME . . . TO . . . SCHOOL now scrolled across the flashing sign. He breathed a sigh of relief.

Veronica laid a hand on his arm. "Look," she said. "I want you to know, I hope I'm wrong about the Gemini. I hope I'm just being . . . paranoid."

"I understand," Fisher said. It was Monday morning. Since Saturday, he and Veronica had barely spoken about the aliens' arrival. They had barely spoken at all. Fisher was still a little hurt that Veronica was being so negative about the single most important event in human history. "Both species just have to work to understand each other."

"Right," Veronica said. But she sounded uncertain.

A few phone calls to the right people and the influence of NASA and the MORONS team had gotten the Gemini permission to take up study at Wompalog in the guise of foreign exchange students. Because Fisher's parents had headed the M3 project, they'd taken responsibility for the well-being of the alien visitors. The bus the Gemini would be living on would stay parked at the Bas residence.

It had taken a significant amount of behind-the-scenes work to create the cover IDs for the Gemini. To ensure they'd be welcome at the school, Principal Teed had received a personal call from the vice president letting him know how important it was that this group of "foreign visitors" would be allowed to take classes at Wompalog. The Independent Federal Republic of Geminolvia was—or so the pamphlet being passed around school read—a tiny nation between Lithuania and Belarus. Most of Fisher's classmates hadn't heard of Lithuania or Belarus, so sticking a made-up country between them wasn't that difficult. To explain the diverse appearance of the Gemini, the country had been described as a tax haven for financial moguls from all corners of the globe. Additionally, the pamphlet read, Geminolvia boasted the highest population of twins in the world.

The stage was set. Principal Teed was standing outside the front doors with an eager crowd of kids waiting to greet the new "foreign exchange students."

Fisher sucked in a deep breath. He just had to make sure that the Gems didn't have the same experience in middle school that he'd had. If that happened, this time tomorrow the whole parking lot would be a smoking mound of charcoal and goop.

A not-too-distant rumble stirred up the eager crowd. The sleek, chrome-trimmed white and gray sides of the Gemini's bus appeared at the far end of the parking lot, eliciting a cheer that spread from one side of the Wompalog crowd to the other.

But as the bus stopped and the door hissed open, silence fell.

The Gemini flowed off the bus as if they were floating. The Gemini greeted their new classmates with waves and dazzling smiles. The girls began whispering and muttering. The boys, by and large, were left mute and wide-eyed, staring at thirteen gorgeous pairs of identical twins.

Wait. Fisher's palms began to sweat. *Thirteen?* Four Gemini had exploded. There should only have been eleven pairs, and twenty-two Gemini. He counted again. Definitely twenty-six.

Before he had time to puzzle this out, Principal Teed stepped up next to the Gemini with a cordless microphone in his hand. He paused in front of the Gemini, making a hesitant offer of his hand before settling on a nod of his head in greeting.

"We at Wompalog are extremely honored and very proud to be a part of this special exchange. We welcome our visitors from the great Independent Federal Republic of, er"—he briefly consulted his notes—"Geminolvia. I know that the bright, kind, and gifted students of this school will give you one of the friendliest welcomes you will find on this planet!"

Fisher chuckled at the principal's choice of words as the students erupted in cheers. He hoped dearly that the Gemini would get a better welcome than he ever had.

The bell rang, signaling it was time for first period, as Principal Teed distributed class schedules to each of the Gemini pairs.

Like everyone else in first period biology, Fisher spent most of his time glancing over at Claire and Deb, Gemini girls Three and Four, studying how they acted and what they said. The boys in particular were hanging on their every word, even if the words weren't anything unusual. Ms. Snapper called on the girls enthusiastically, not missing the chance to educate special guests.

"Now," Ms. Snapper said, "who can tell me the different functions of B and T cells in the human immune system?"

Ms. Snapper scanned the classroom. Claire glanced cautiously left and right. Fisher nearly choked as her arm became *longer*. Just a few inches—too small a change for anyone besides Fisher to notice. But the change had the desired effect. Ms. Snapper promptly beamed at her.

"Claire?"

"Well," Claire said, "first of all, they work a lot like the immune cells of the wild Eight-Fanged Mud-Dancer of Tixtillorsk Seven—"

"*Lake!*" Fisher jumped in before Claire could go on. "Lake Tixtillorsk Seven, in Geminolvia. Claire was just telling me about it before class. Named, of course, for the great General Tixtillorsk, who, uh, was so great that naming one or two or six lakes after him just wasn't enough."

He heard his own breathing in his ears as the room went silent and everyone's attention turned from the Gemini to him. They seemed to have bought it. If anything, they were just annoyed that someone other than Claire had spoken.

"Well, thank you for the background, Fisher," Ms. Snapper said. "Please go on, Claire."

The rest of Claire's answer was a perfectly ordinary description of B and T cells and contained no further references to planets nobody'd ever heard of. Still, Fisher realized he might soon find himself explaining some very strange facts about the wildlife in Geminolvia.

One period down. As Fisher headed to math, he saw four of the Gemini standing with the Vikings by a bank of temporary lockers that had been shipped in along with the trailers. Apparently, the Gemini had forgiven the Vikings for being massive wastes of carbon and hydrogen, and the Vikings had apparently forgiven the Gemini for nearly blowing them into nanovikings.

Brody and Leroy were shuffling their feet, and their hands hung at their sides like freshly caught grouper fish. Willard was telling the Gemini all about his rocket scientist dad and his work at NASA.

"It really is very s-simple," he said. "B-Beethoven's Fifth Law says that an object at rest will stay indoors, ex-except after C," he said. "Or C minor."

Fisher kept walking. The Gemini, he thought, looked amused—kind of like a person watching a dog trying to carry a long stick through a narrow door over and over again.

Math went smoothly, until the last twenty-five minutes, when Anna and Bee recited the first three thousand digits of pi. Fisher had heard experts recite a thousand pi digits before, but he'd never seen two people go back and forth, not making a single error and in perfect rhythm, until the class was nearly hypnotized.

As Bee spoke the three thousandth digit, the bell rang for lunch.

"Brava!" Mr. Taggart, the math teacher, burst into enthusiastic applause before dismissing the class. "Truly remarkable. Thank you, girls."

Fisher was getting increasingly confident as the day went on. The Gemini were a hit—and he'd seen no signs of their earlier *explosive* tendencies.

He might actually be able to pull this off.

Fisher and Alex shepherded Anna and Bee through the trailers that currently made up Wompalog. The school had set up a temporary cafeteria under a tent, but Fisher and Alex weren't going to subject the Gemini to Wompalog food and risk another fiery display of temper. Instead, they guided the extraterrestrial visitors to the one redeeming feature of their parking lot school's existence: the King of Hollywood.

As usual, the KOH was flooded by the Wompalog population at lunchtime, with a line out the door. Rather than stand in line, however, Bee and Anna walked immediately to the soda station, and grabbed a huge handful of cup lids. Then they marched up to the counter. The kids in line still marveled at the sight of them and let them cut ahead without complaint. They didn't even seem to notice the lid collection.

"All of these, please," said Anna, indicating the lids.

"Er . . . okay!" said the woman behind the counter, radiating confusion. "What size do you want the drinks?"

"We get drinks with them?" said Bee with a giant smile.

Fisher scurried up to the cashier, and explained that the girls were from Geminolvia and things were very different there. He then pointed out the wall menu to the Gemini, and soon he, Alex, Anna, and Bee, had loaded up trays with delectable grilled and fried Earth cuisine.

They took their lunch to a big, round table. Alex pattered ahead, set his tray down, and pulled out a chair for Bee, who graciously accepted. Alex, instead of sitting down himself, pulled his chair into the middle of the room.

"All right!" he said, hopping up on the chair and tapping a plastic cup with a plastic spoon to indicate a toast was coming. "Ladies and gentlemen, boys and girls, today is a very special day." He beamed in the direction of the Gemini.

"Our guests"—he indicated them with a sweep of his right hand—"have traveled a very long way to be here. They could have chosen any spot on this planet . . . er, continent . . . as their destination. They have chosen *our* spot." Applause began in a few areas around the room. "So let's make sure they have, truly, the best day on Earth."

He winked knowingly at Anna and Bee, who winked in return. The applause broke out in full force, accented by cheers, whoops, and shouts. Fortunately, all the noise and excitement prevented the students from remarking on the fact that the Gemini were busy devouring their spicy fries—boxes included.

Fisher's happiness was disrupted only once, when Amanda and Veronica sailed through the doors, glared first at Fisher, then at Alex, and then at the Gemini, and deliberately took a seat in the opposite corner of the room. Fisher was starting to get frustrated. Maybe the girls thought he and Alex were being too trusting too soon. But how were they supposed to build a diplomatic relationship if they didn't extend all courtesy to the Gemini? As awful as Veronica's glare felt, Fisher had to stomach it. The future of human–extraterrestrial relations was more important.

After lunch was phys ed. The gym was the only portion of Wompalog that hadn't been badly damaged in the final battle with Three.

When Fisher emerged from the locker room, the Gemini were already assembled, in identical blue shorts and T-shirts. Amanda was glaring at them, arms crossed.

"They didn't even go into the locker room," Amanda muttered. "They just ducked into a side hallway and *transformed*. If anyone else had seen, they would've been busted."

"We'll tell them to be more careful," Fisher whispered

back. He was just relieved Amanda was talking to him. Not so with Veronica. She was sitting on the bleachers, deliberately avoiding eye contact. He cleared his throat. "I think today's gone pretty well so far, don't you?"

Amanda shot him a dirty look and merely grunted.

"Okay! The sport of the day is dodgeball," announced Mr. Wells, the massive gym teacher, brushing a hand across his blond bristle.

"Um," Fisher said, "I'm not sure if that's really—"

"We don't know that much about your sports," said Bee, cutting him off. "But we're familiar with the rules of your 'dodgeball.' We would be honored to participate in your athletic custom."

"I agree," Amanda said, adjusting her prescription athletic goggles. "It's a great idea." Fisher didn't like the look on her face *at all*. "In fact . . . there are twenty-six Wompalog students in this class. There are twenty-six Gemini. In the spirit of healthy competition and mutual entertainment, why don't we make it an interstell . . . an *international* contest?"

Mr. Wells beamed. "I think that would be a fine way to welcome our guests," he said. "Let's try it!"

Cheers went up from the human students. The Gemini nodded in unsettling unison.

Amanda was cracking her knuckles as she stretched her calves and tested her still-recovering ankle. She gave the Gemini a grin that showed a bit too many of her teeth. Fisher had seen that look at the beginning of every one of Amanda's wrestling matches.

"Do you really think competition is a good idea?" Fisher said to Alex as the teams lined up and started picking up the rubber dodgeballs. The Gemini looked at their balls like they were contemplating how good they would be with a side of hash browns.

"Why not?" Alex said. "This could pave the way for Galactic Olympics, or a Many Worlds Cup! Think of the possib-*ouuumphh*!" He was cut off as a dodgeball ricocheted off his head, dropping him faster than a wrecking ball covered in tranquilizer darts.

The onslaught began.

The Gemini worked together like they had planned every move and practiced for years. They shifted positions fluidly, one ducking just as another leapt over her, two exchanging places with a single sidestep to dodge incoming throws and deliver precise counter-throws. The Wompalog kids ran back and forth in disarray as the incoming projectiles arrived with incredible speed and sent them crashing to the floor or sailing off their feet.

They were dropping like very uncoordinated, panicky flies.

Fisher was finally lining up a throw on Kat when Leigh sent a shot straight at his right ear. His ears started to ring and his knees simply gave out, as if they'd been vaporized.

He looked around as he sank to the floor. Amanda was fuming. Alex was still clutching his head. Erin's lanky frame was splayed out on the ground like a tackled spider.

"Round one, Gemini!" said Mr. Wells. "Take a minute, then line up for round two."

"VICTORY!" shouted all the Gemini together.

Alex crawled over to Fisher.

"*Still* think this was a good idea?" Fisher said.

"Sure do," Alex said, gasping. "I actually came prepared for just such a situation." He picked himself off the ground and then limped over to a duffel bag sitting to the bleachers. From it, he pulled out a thick handful of translucent plastic.

"Are those my strength-enhancing sleeves? The ones I've been working on in *secret*?" Fisher said pointedly, emphasizing *secret*. Alex acted as if he hadn't heard. As soon as Mr. Wells was bent over the water fountain, Alex called a huddle and began distributing the sleeves to his teammates.

Fisher scrambled to his feet and yanked Alex back from the crowd. "I only made four of them," Fisher whispered. "Prototypes."

"Mm-hm," Alex said, sliding one of the sleeves onto his right arm and flexing his fingers.

[TOP SECRET!!!]
STRENGTH SLEEVES

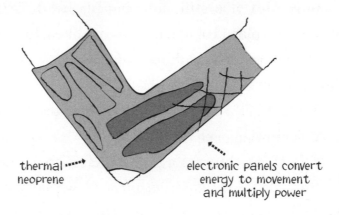

thermal ·····▸
neoprene

◂·····
electronic panels convert
energy to movement
and multiply power

TRANSPARENT STATE

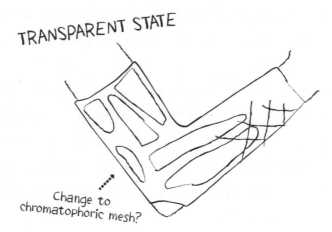

◂·····
Change to
chromatophoric mesh?

"You stole one and duplicated them!" Fisher said.

"Seems like you've figured everything out by yourself," Alex said, pulling the last of the sleeves onto Fisher's arms. "Just suit up, 'kay?"

Fisher complied, sighing. Just because they got along now didn't mean the old Two was gone. Sometimes, Alex's unpredictability had saved Fisher's life, and sometimes it filled him with the urge to throw his clone off a house and into a swimming pool full of mustard.

Alex had made an important modification to Fisher's design—after stealing it, Fisher thought grumpily. The sleeves took on the skin tone of their wearers, becoming nearly invisible once worn.

"Ready?" said Mr. Wells. His whistle shrieked, and the second battle was on.

This time, the students had the firepower they needed. The Gemini were caught totally off guard. They couldn't dodge the much-faster balls, which whistled through the air like cannon fire.

Fisher ducked under a bright green ball, cocked his right arm back like a baseball pitcher's, and slung his orange ball at Bee with a stinging *whishhhhh!* Bee tried to sidestep, but his augmented throw tagged her right on the ribs, and she staggered and finally collapsed to the floor. Amanda took a two-step windup, hurling her own orb of rubbery destruction from a full backward extension like a javelin. Anna took the shot on her left hip and flailed, balance gone, until she landed right on top of Bee. A sinister grin curled Amanda's lip.

Fisher picked up another ball and searched for a new

target. As he held the dodgeball up in a ready position, his bicep twitched. Unfortunately, the sleeve augmented the muscle movement, making Fisher's arm thrash sideways and slam the ball into his own head.

As Fisher stumbled, he noticed other kids having similar problems. The sleeves were very powerful, but they weren't fine-tuned. Alex had taken and copied them before Fisher had had time to properly test them. Every few seconds a dodgeball would go flying in a completely random direction.

Despite the malfunctioning sleeves, however, in the end, the humans narrowly prevailed. The Gemini sat or lay on the floor, looks of utter shock on their faces, as the human students let out cheers and excited whoops.

"Round two to Wompalog!" Mr. Wells said. "I knew you just needed to warm up a little. Okay, we can take a water break if you . . . " He stopped, tilting his head, and his nose began to twitch. "What is that sound? Is—is somebody making *popcorn*?"

Oh, no, thought Fisher, *not again.*

BOOM.

What was left of Mae and Nina had turned a section of the bleachers into a spray of mulch and an enormous puff of sawdust. A thin layer of green glop coated a fair amount of the gym floor. A girl named Kiera was screaming as the other kids flattened themselves to the ground, clearly assuming they were under attack. Mr. Wells had fallen over, partly from the blast wave, but mostly from surprise. He popped up quickly, doing a rapid check to make sure everyone was all right.

Fisher put his arms around his knees and bowed his head. Sirens were audible in less than a minute.

The Gemini smoothed their hair in unison.

"We would like to play a different game," said Anna, smiling.

CHAPTER 7

The primary motivator of every organism is survival.
The primary obstacle to survival, often enough, is
another organism. This fact is responsible for everything
interesting about life.
                    —Dr. X, "Thoughts on Human Weakness"

"This whole situation is hovering an inch from disaster," Fisher said gloomily as he and Alex trudged home from school. "How did this happen?" He kicked angrily at a pile of leaves.

"We weren't ready for the Gemini, pure and simple," Alex said, his right hand tapping a nervous rhythm against his right leg. "If Mom and Dad had warned us the Gemini were coming, maybe we could've prepared."

"I doubt it," Fisher grumbled.

The Bas boys had taken the fall for the explosion in the gym. They'd confessed to using strength-enhancing sleeves and claimed that an external power generator to which they were wirelessly connected must have over-loaded. There were so many Gemini, no one had noticed that two of them had been incinerated by the blast.

Because nobody had been hurt, the fire department

had simply confiscated the sleeves, but the fire chief had sternly said that Fisher and Alex could expect to hear from the police soon. Meanwhile, Principal Teed had gotten word and was deliberating on their suspension.

Alex's phone buzzed in his pocket. He put it to his ear, listened, and groaned.

"Voice mail from Mom," he said, slipping it back into his pocket. "She and Dad went to a research lab at Stanford this afternoon to do more work on the Gemini. She said that we shouldn't expect them back tonight. I don't think the principal got hold of them before they left. *Supposedly*, the Gemini will be confined to their bus until they get back." Alex made it clear that he thought the possibility unlikely.

But Fisher felt a flare-up of hope. "That gives us time to plan," Fisher said as the cluster of antennae on top of their house appeared over the rooftops. "I think we need to change our approach."

"What we need is to give the Gemini an actual education," Alex said. "We need to teach them what things are like on Earth and why you can't just blow up when you get annoyed."

In the house, Fisher and Alex kicked off their shoes like they were stinging insects. Fisher felt like he'd lived two whole lifetimes since the morning. FP romped down the hall from the kitchen, trailing the remains of a torn-apart cereal box from his tail, and started nuzzling Fisher's ankles with happy snorts.

Paul ambled on his tentacles down the stairs and gave Alex a few friendly pats. Alex looked at Fisher.

"All right," said Fisher. "Time for some serious planning. We need mind fuel."

"Guacamole?" said Alex.

"You know it," said Fisher.

They trekked into the kitchen. Fisher grabbed a big bag of tortilla chips from the pantry and Alex walked up to the fridge.

"Hey, fridge," Alex said.

"Greetings, Alexander," said the fridge in a pleasant, mellow, female voice. It had made a point to be especially courteous since its brief rebellion caused by Three's chaos signal.

"Is there any guacamole left from last night?" Alex asked.

"Yes," said the fridge. "You can find it next to the milk on the lowest shelf. I have kept it at optimal temperature. Your mother also requests that you take care not to jostle the middle shelf. She is incubating a semi-intelligent micro-arboreal fungivore."

"Oh yeah," Alex said. "The scum-eating fridge tree. She really hates scrubbing you." He opened the door and swiped a little Tupperware container from inside.

"Most cheerful greetings to you both, my dear boys!" the toaster piped up in his posh English accent. "I trust your day was a success in every regard?"

Lord Burnside sat happily on the countertop, like any other toaster but with much greater poise and refinement. He was capable of very sophisticated conversation but his dreams remained the same: achieving the ideal crunchiness on the topmost layer of a slice of bread.

"Not so much in the lack-of-explosions regard, Lord Burnside," said Alex, sitting down next to Fisher at the kitchen table and popping the lid off the guacamole as Fisher opened the chips.

"Oh dear," Lord Burnside said, the glowing spots that served as his eyes dipped in sympathy. After a moment they took a quizzical bend. "Perhaps it is merely my lack of expertise in any other realm than the crisping of whole wheat slices, but it seems that large explosions occur with unusual frequency in your lives. Is this typical?"

"Not quite," said Fisher, scooping up a healthy amount of the dip with his first chip.

"So what do we do?" Alex asked, the question muffled by a full mouth of chips. "How can we establish a diplomatic relationship with the Gemini when we never know what might literally set them off?"

"Knowledge is always the key," Fisher said, leaning back in his chair. "We need to understand them in order to make this arrangement work. And *they* need to understand *us*. As much as they've studied us from up in space, they're clearly missing some important points about human interaction." He sighed. "We need to clear up some things with them before they come back to Wompalog. I mean, it's obvious they *mean* well—"

They heard the front door open.

"Huh," Fisher said. "I guess Mom and Dad came back early."

Alex's eyes widened. "Not unless Mom and Dad sound like half the kids at Wompalog," Alex leapt to his feet and dashed out of the kitchen. Fisher heard the growing babble of voices and raced to the front hallway.

Kids were pouring in the front door. A high percentage of the seventh grade, plus some sixth and eighth graders. Before Fisher or Alex could react, the house was full.

"How'd they get through the gate?" Fisher shouted.

At the center of the throng were the Gemini.

"Fisher," Alex said, tapping the screen near the door to bring up the front gate camera.

"What the . . . " Fisher said, staring at the image of Zoe standing in the Liquid Door to keep it open and waving in a few stragglers from school.

"How is it opening for her?" Fisher said, then noticed a small object in Zoe's hand. "Is that . . . is that a comb?"

Alex patted his back pocket.

"Yes," he said. *"My* comb. Mental note, the genetic scanner of the Liquid Door is hypersensitive and needs serious adjustments."

"We'll have to get on that if our house is still standing tomorrow," Fisher groaned.

"What's going on?" shouted Alex above the clamor, stepping forward to confront the Gemini.

"What's it look like?" asked Bee. "Everyone at Wompalog's got so much work to do. Stress is a killer, am I right?"

Bee and Anna executed a perfect fist bump. *A fist bump?* Fisher thought.

"We decided to invite them over for a little fun!" Bee went on.

"I thought—"Alex's eyes were ticking back and forth frantically, like a metronome gone wild. He gulped. "But what about staying on the bus?"

Anna rolled her eyes and lowered her voice. "We traveled two thousand light-years in a ship to get here! We're tired of sitting still. Besides—" she sniffed disdainfully. "The bus doesn't even have Wi-Fi!"

"Wait!" Fisher said, snatching a vase out of George Katz's hand, which he'd been about to use as a football to hurl across the living room. "We can't throw parties here! This house is full of experimental technology and potentially dangerous lab equipment!"

Anna and Bee merely shrugged and pushed past them.

"Wait!" Fisher called again. But they were already gone.

He followed four of the Gemini from somewhere in the middle of the alphabet into the kitchen and found the fridge flung wide open.

"Stop!" he said. "That's our food!"

It was too late. They'd cleaned out the fridge in a matter of seconds. Fisher spotted the fridge tree crawling away by its little branches and managed to grab it before it became Gemini salad.

"Enough," he said. "If you're that hungry, you should . . . what are you still eating, anyway?" The food was gone, but the Gemini still had their mouths full. "Never mind," Fisher said. "Just . . . don't move. I'll be back."

Fisher deposited the fridge tree in a small cupboard in the hallway and tried to put together a plan to round everyone up and get them out the door.

The party was already in full swing. Fisher's barely renewed hope was plunged back into arctic waters. The Gemini didn't want to talk. They didn't seem to want a cultural exchange at all. They just wanted to dress up and treat the human world like a dollhouse. An easily explodable, flammable dollhouse. Alex had his hands clasped behind his head in frustration.

"Fisher, even *I* don't know a bunch of these kids," Alex

said, turning in slow circles and taking in the crowd.

Fisher's mind was racing. "A head-on confrontation is a bad idea," he said, miming an explosion with his hands.

"No kidding," Alex answered. "Let's work on the kids first and get to the Gemini when everyone else is out the door."

Fisher nodded. "You take the upstairs. I'll stay down here."

Alex gave him the thumbs-up and bolted up the stairs.

In the kitchen, the Gemini were setting out trays full of snacks. Fisher had no idea where they'd gotten more food, but if there was anything strange or untrustworthy about the choice of edibles, it was too late to warn the students, or FP, who was going through the party mix faster than fire through gasoline-soaked matchbooks.

Three eighth graders were marveling over the automatic self-setting dining table, whose instantly extracting arms could move with great speed and handle a variety of utensils. One of them had discovered the automated features by accident when he'd dropped his glass and the table shot out an arm to catch it. Now all three students were tossing plates and glasses in the air to watch the table grab at them.

It was only a matter of time before something broke— or worse, someone got clocked in the face by an overenthusiastic table arm. Fisher realized this might be just the time for a field test of his newest device.

During the infiltration of TechX to hunt down the evil Dr. X, Fisher had used his Memory Loop serum to make a guard experience the same six seconds over and over. It was like replacing a live security camera feed with a repeating tape. Recently, Fisher had been experimenting on a new variety of the serum. Its purpose was to distract FP when Fisher had important work to do. Unfortunately, the serum was as of yet untested.

The kids laughed maniacally as they tossed more and more plates, forks, serving platters, and glasses at the table. Fisher knew the table was reaching its capacity. He had no choice. He would have to act fast. Soon, the arms would start missing, and plates—or bones—would start shattering.

Fisher pulled a small plastic pellet out of his pocket and hurled it at the kitchen floor. Its thin plastic shell broke open, releasing a fine powder in a cloud that Fisher was just outside of, as per his exact calculations.

Instantly, the kids stopped what they were doing, smiled, and sat down.

Fisher nearly laughed out loud. It was working! He knew that right now each kid was recalling the experience of eating a favorite food in such exquisite detail that he would stay occupied for at least another half hour . . . when the serum wore off.

But Fisher couldn't relax yet. In the living room, Chance Barrows, the multisport star and glowing pinnacle of cool among seventh-grade boys, had just tripped over the release lever for the tank holding Mr. Bas's collective-mind ants. The entire swarm shared a single mind, and it flowed out of the tank like a wave. Chance dove out of the way as the ants searched for food. The swarm moved in absolute unison, perfect coordination, taking sharp turns and twists as they headed for the kitchen.

Chance crushed a few dozen as he clambered out of the way, but the hive continued on like nothing had happened. Fisher raced for the pantry, holding his breath as he passed through the kitchen, where some of the memory serum powder was no doubt still lingering in the air. Finally, he found the emergency ant containment device: a Dustbuster with "Emergency Ant Containment Device" written on it in black Sharpie.

The ants preferred food but they didn't mind consuming other things—much like the Gemini, Fisher thought. They'd already begun chewing up the living room carpet, and if left to their own devices would go straight through the hardwood floor. If they reached the outdoors, they could wreck the local environment.

"Sweet party trick!" said a short boy Fisher didn't know, his eyes following the ant swarm like it was a light show. Chance had hopped up onto the couch.

NOTES ON
MEMORY
SERUM PELLETS

PURPOSE: to distract FP

FORMULA: variation on
Memory Loop serum

DELIVERY METHOD: PELLET

OBSERVATIONS and SIDE EFFECTS:
• need to program other foods for
additional applications—not everyone
likes popcorn as much as FP

• blissful state potentially
entertaining for bystanders, therein
a new distraction?

• too long-lasting, may dilute

"Yeah, thanks!" Fisher squawked out as he desperately grabbed a plate full of donuts off the coffee table and hurled it on the carpet. As the ants swarmed over the food, Fisher hopped back and forth with the E.A.C.D. on full power. Working as fast as he could, he was able to suck up most of insects. He marched back to the tank, made sure the lever was reset to "closed," opened a small chute at the top, and knocked the ants back into their proper home.

"Master Fisher! Master Fisher!" came Burnside's high voice from the kitchen, and Fisher ran to the aid of his loyal toaster and friend, once again keeping his hand cupped over his mouth as he passed the kitchen table.

He pushed his way through a throng of students crowded around the counter, where he found Yang and Zoe gnawing on Lord Burnside's cord like it was a piece of licorice. Around them was a pile of partly eaten plates and mugs with huge bites taken out of them. Clearly, when the Gemini ran out of food in the kitchen they decided to cut out the middle step and just eat the kitchen.

"Hey!" Fisher said, yanking the toaster cord out of their hands. The two Gemini looked at him with mild confusion.

"We were eating that!" Yang said.

"We're hungry," Zoe said.

"I'm sorry," Fisher said, trying to sound pleasant and not one second away from a total breakdown. "This is a part of Lord Burnside." He patted the toaster. "He . . . helps prepare consumables. It would be a much better use of him to make toast."

"Toast!" said Yang excitedly.

"What's that?" said Zoe. The Gemini, Fisher noted, had some very significant gaps in their human knowledge.

"I'll show you," Fisher said.

There was a hidden cupboard that even the voracious Gemini hadn't found. Lord Burnside got very antsy when the bread supply ran out, and so Mr. and Mrs. Bas kept an emergency stash. And this was definitely an emergency. Fisher reached in for the package of bread, put two slices into Lord Burnside, and pulled down his lever. "In a minute or two, those will be crispy."

"Perfectly," Burnside added in a slightly quivering voice. Clearly, he'd been traumatized by the fact that he'd very nearly been devoured.

"We shall consume your toast," said Zoe, sounding less like a teen girl, and much more like Principal Teed trying to get control of the school after Ice Cream Day.

"*All* of it," said Yang with an intensity normally reserved for serious medical diagnoses and *Hamlet* monologues.

Another crisis avoided, Fisher jogged out of the

kitchen and upstairs, where Alex was trying to keep everyone away from their parents' personal labs. Their automatic security systems didn't ask any questions before releasing a cloud of forty-eight-hour sleeping gas, and some of the kids were getting dangerously close to setting them off.

Something else was bothering him, too—he hadn't kept an exact count, but he was positive not all of the Gemini were in the house. There were at least three or four pairs unaccounted for. What were the others up to? Was something even bigger coming?

Whatever it was, he'd have to deal with the Gemini one crisis at a time. The party had to be shut down. Alex took a moment to catch his breath when he saw Fisher running up.

"How's it going up here?" Fisher said, mopping sweat from his forehead with his sleeve.

"Not great," Alex said. "I'm shoving people toward the doors as fast as I can, but as soon as I move on to the next group they come right back. We need help."

"Who's gonna help us?" Fisher said. "Everyone loves the Gemini!"

Alex let out a long sigh.

"Not *everyone*," he said pointedly.

Fisher blinked as Alex's meaning settled on him like the cold, clammy touch of a wet bathing suit. But he knew he had no choice. He swallowed. "I'll ask," he said.

"You'll plead," Alex corrected.

Fisher closed the upstairs bathroom door behind him and pulled out his phone, dialing Veronica's number with shaking fingers.

≋ CHAPTER 8 ≋

My patience is equal to five hundred straws. And that—
that was the last one.

—Prince Xultar of Venus,
sworn enemy of Vic Daring, Issue #38

Ten minutes later, Amanda kicked open the front door
with such force that it smacked into Jacob Li, making
him spill his fruit punch into a luckily placed bowl of corn
chips. Amanda and Veronica stepped through the hallway
and into the living room simultaneously, smoothly taking
off identical pairs of sunglasses.

"All right," Amanda said, cracking her knuckles. "This
party is over."

Five Gemini pairs turned to look at her with a unified swivel of their necks. Their silky hair fell gracefully
across their shoulders.

Everyone else in the room also turned after a split second. All with the same blank, mysterious eyes.

Alien eyes, you could call them.

"Fisher . . . " Alex muttered.

"Yeah," Fisher said. "I see it."

The other kids *were* Gemini.

Fisher wanted to turn invisible, back out of the room, and seal it shut. He should have seen this coming. The Gemini could take any form they wanted. And it had become very clear that they'd started as beautiful girls because they knew it would make people like them more, trust them more, and pay less attention to all the strange things they'd started to do. But they could look like anything. They could blend in to the human population. They could do anything they wanted and nobody would know it was them.

"We do not wish to end the party," said one of the Gemini in the corner, who looked sort of like Chance—a big, athletic boy with wavy blond hair.

"Well, this isn't your house," said Veronica. "Or, furthermore, your planet. We've tolerated your impish antics thus far, but you're taxing our hospitality to its furthest extremes. Your welcome is wearing tenuously thin."

The Gemini cocked their heads slightly at Veronica's speech.

"Advanced vocabulary," Anna muttered, shaking her head a little. "We're having difficulty interpreting that statement."

"Try interpreting *this*," Amanda said, and in three large steps had reached the jock-looking Gemini. She put a foot into the side of his knee and he collapsed to the floor. Amanda stood over him and locked his left arm behind his back with one hand, her other hand pulling his head back by the hair.

"Now," Veronica said. "Go back to your little bus."

"Very well," one of the Gemini on the couch spoke up. But before she'd finished saying "well," an explosion shook the windows. Fisher, Alex, Veronica, and Amanda turned to see a fireball pluming up from Mrs. Bas's garden. The Gemini stood up, as one unit, and left, the disguised ones gradually shifting back into their original girl forms as they walked.

Alex rushed to the window.

"Nobody's hurt," he said. "Looks like one of the Gemini was exploring the garden—"

"Eating the garden, you mean?" Fisher interjected, gesturing to the giant cornstalk, which had been chewed to bits *and* flattened by a giant blast.

Alex nodded.

"Poor Fee," Fisher sighed. Charred vegetable matter now mixed with Gemini glop in the smoking brown grass. He turned away from the window, frowning. Something wasn't right. Or rather, something was even less right than the fact that a bunch of aliens had just thrown a party in his house and nearly incinerated his mom's garden.

There was no *way* the Gemini in the garden had overheard Veronica and Amanda demanding that the Gemini leave. All the windows had been closed. And yet the explosion had come only moments after Amanda had declared the party over. It was almost as if . . .

"By the protractor of Pythagoras," Fisher said. "I know what the Gemini are."

Amanda narrowed his eyes at him. "You mean other than a bunch of vicious, porcelain-eating predators?"

Fisher ignored her. Other students were still clustered in the living room. It wasn't yet safe to talk. Now that the Gemini were gone, however, it didn't take long to shepherd the other kids out of the house. One by one, Amanda ushered the students to the door, smiling menacingly and cracking her knuckles whenever she encountered any resistance.

"Phew. That's the last of them," Fisher said, closing the front door and sagging against it.

"Not quite," Alex said. He pointed down the hallway to the kitchen, where three kids were still sitting at the dining table, staring into space. *Oops.* Fisher had forgotten about the memory serum. He searched around for the counteragent, hoping he'd made enough for all of them. It wasn't in the drawer he thought he'd put it in, and he was about to give up and hope the stuff wore off when Paul sidled up to him, holding a small plastic case in an outstretched tentacle.

"Oh . . . thank you, Paul," Fisher said, petting the little octopus. "I . . . don't know how you knew I needed this, but it's not the weirdest thing that's happened today by a long stretch."

Fisher tossed a pellet with the counteragent to his memory serum at the feet of the three kids. As they shook themselves out of their stupor, Fisher, Alex, and Veronica led them out of their chairs and out the door.

Once the party had *officially* disbanded, Fisher gestured Alex, Veronica, and Amanda over to the ant farm, where hundreds of ants were busily tending to their ant business, seamlessly organized into different task forces, controlled by unified instinct.

"Strictly speaking," Fisher said excitedly, "the Gemini aren't a *they* at all. The Gemini are a *single being*. It can divide itself into many physical pieces but they share the same consciousness. One mind."

"Of course," Alex said, snapping his fingers. "No wonder they act together so well. Each of its human shapes is just an extension of one will. When one of them blows up it doesn't really matter to the creature as a whole."

"So that's why the Gemini in the garden blew up . . . " Veronica said. "She didn't *hear* the conversation. She just . . . knew about it."

Amanda shivered. "Creepy."

"Another thing," Fisher said. "They keep blowing up but their numbers stay the same. They can *regrow* their shapes."

"But not right away," said Veronica slowly. "After one

explodes, the Gemini must have to regain energy to make new ones. Maybe that's why they eat so much. What happens when they start making new drones faster than they explode?"

"That means there's no telling how fast this thing could grow," said Amanda as they moved through the living room, plumping couch cushions, cleaning up spilled drinks, and searching for any stray ants. "For all we know it could keep growing and eating until Gemini drones outnumber humans. With enough time they could turn the whole planet into a desert."

All four of them were silent for nearly a minute as they imagined Earth as a dried-up husk covered in Gemini drones.

Alex shook his head. "We won't let that happen," he said determinedly.

"What are we going to do to prevent it?" Veronica said.

"First," Fisher pointed out, "we can start by cleaning up. We won't be doing much of *anything* if we get grounded for wrecking the house."

After another hour of picking up, tossing, scrubbing, and vacuuming, the house was spotless. And just in time. The whispery hum and sweet smell of the car's corn syrup-powered engine announced Mr. and Mrs. Bas's return.

"Oh boy," said Alex. "Okay, let's go try and explain the crater that used to be Mom's garden." He nodded at

Fisher. "Will you two wait in Fisher's room so we can make a plan for dealing with the Gems?"

"All right," Amanda said. She and Veronica went upstairs, followed by FP, as the Bas boys walked out to the front yard.

There was still a thin smoke trail curling up from the garden. In addition to Fee, the garden had previously boasted a collection of string beans the size of small trees. Two of them were in tiny fragments and the other four had been felled, with charred spots mottling the green.

Mrs. Bas's face turned white as soon as she stepped out of the car. "How?" was all she said.

"The Gemini threw a party without asking us," said Fisher, deciding honesty might be best.

Mr. Bas clasped his hands behind his back, solemnly surveying the wreckage.

"The house was in danger," said Alex. "We tried to keep things under control but it was too much to handle. We had to kick them out. They didn't like that. And so . . ." He gestured weakly at the garden.

Mrs. Bas looked at the garden, then back at the boys.

"Well . . . " she said in a thin voice, "I guess it's just lucky that nobody got hurt."

"And I guess dinner's already cooked," said Mr. Bas, pointing to the charred plant life. "But I'm afraid we won't be at the table. We've got a lot of work to do tonight.

We've made an important discovery about Gemini neuro-biology. They're—"

"A hive mind," Alex said before Mr. Bas could finish. "We figured that out, too, from their behavior. And they're starting to take on new forms. They could be trying to blend in with us."

"We think . . . maybe they came to Earth to do more than just study us," Fisher said slowly, though he hated to even think the words, much less say them out loud. We think maybe they came here to . . . " He swallowed. "Eat."

The parents looked at each other grimly.

"They're a potential threat to us, no question," Mr. Bas said. "We'll have to deal with that threat cautiously. And we need to do more research before we decide what has to be done."

"In the meanwhile, try to be nice to them," Mrs. Bas said. "The less they think we know, the better position we're in. And remember, you two: bringing them here was our idea, and our responsibility. We tracked them, we built the M3." She put her arm through her husband's, and took a deep, shuddering breath. "It's up to us to fix this."

They took a step toward the front door when Mrs. Bas's pocket buzzed. She held up her phone.

"Blocked number," she said, putting it to her ear. "Hello? Yes, this is . . . " A stony paleness spread across her face. "Yes, sir. Understood. We'll be there." She hung up. "That was the chairman of the Joint Chiefs of Staff at the Pentagon. They need us to attend a meeting at once."

"Where?" Alex said. "About the Gemini?"

"He wouldn't tell me over the phone," she said. "But several other leading scientists, the secretaries of defense and state, and the president are going to be there. He said that a car would be . . . " Before she could finish the thought, the low growl of a powerful engine was heard outside the front yard's wall. "That's our ride."

"Keep your eyes on the Gemini," Mr. Bas said. "We'll be back as soon as we can." The look in his eyes made it clear that, as much as he was trying to hide it, he didn't really have any idea when that might be. Fisher's parents disappeared through the front gate.

"Well," Alex said, "that's a little strange. Maybe they'll figure out exactly what they need to do."

"Maybe," Fisher said darkly, "but I'd rather not wait to find out. We need to have a meeting of our own, or it's going to get a lot worse."

Upstairs, Veronica and Amanda were perched on Fisher's windowsill. Fisher closed the door behind him as Alex sank into Fisher's bed.

"Do you have anything to say to us?" Amanda said, crossing her arms.

Fisher looked at Alex. Alex nodded. "We're sorry," Fisher

G = growth rate for Gemini Girls

$$\left(\frac{F}{m} \right)^{\frac{1}{t}} - x = G$$

let:

x = probability of exploding spontaneously

F = pounds of "food*" eaten in kg
  (includes plastic, paper products, porcelain)

t = time in hours

m = theoretical Gemini metabolic
  rate in kJ/hour

  *study eating habits of goats,
  ants???

said, picking up FP and looking at his still-tender ear. He gave the pig a scratch under the chin. "We wanted to believe that aliens were enlightened. That they were friendly."

"That they had answers," Alex added.

"What you wanted," Veronica said, with a softer tone than Fisher had expected, "was for aliens to be just like humans, but kinder."

"So how do we get rid of them?" Amanda said, cutting straight to the part of the conversation Fisher had been afraid to reach. "Can we make them so angry they all blow up at once? If *none* of the drones can eat, maybe they can't gather up enough energy to regenerate."

"That'd be dangerous," said Alex. "The force of the blast might be exponential. Thousands of people could die."

"Maybe we can convince them there are greener pastures elsewhere," said Fisher. "If they realize Earth is going to be more trouble than it's worth, they might move on."

"If I may, kids?" said CURTIS as Fisher's computer screen popped into life. Ever since Fisher had rescued the artificial intelligence from TechX, he'd proven quite capable, and at times indispensable. "That could be a tough proposition. I've been lookin' at the MORONS research, and it looks like the Gemini ship took a big hit when it crashed. Definitely fixable, but it's not at the park anymore."

"Maybe your parents could help us find it," Amanda said.

"Our parents just got whisked away by a mystery car to a secret meeting with the president," Alex said. "I tried calling them both a minute ago just to see if it would work. Signal's blocked."

"Figured that," Fisher said. "I got NASA's number after the Gemini landed. Maybe we can try them." He dialed the number and put his phone on speaker.

"Welcome to NASA," an automated voice said. "If you are calling to inquire about satellite launch services, press one. If you wish to contribute to the next robotic mission to Mars, press two. If you are a robot on Mars, press three. If you have other business, press four. If you are attempting to reach the Nautical Armwrestling Society of Alaska, please hang up and try again."

Fisher shrugged and pressed four.

"Thank you," the voice picked back up after a moment. "If your business is related to current space missions, press one. If it is related to NASA publicity or tourism, press two. If you are an astronaut from the future who has risked everything in a last-ditch attempt to avert global disaster, please stay on the line for appropriate dramatic music."

Fisher jabbed the end call button as an orchestra swelled into an adventurous theme.

"By the time that becomes helpful we'd have been up to our hair in Gemini drones," Veronica sighed.

"Now what?" said Amanda.

"I just called Agent Mason while that was going on," Alex said. "But the call didn't connect."

"Where could he be?" Fisher said. "And how else are we going to find the ship?"

"Ahem!" CURTIS said. "I think I may be of assistance. During that call I took the liberty of using your phone connection to hack into NASA's mainframe. I got the ship's location. They took it to a secret NASA facility. It's only a couple of miles from here."

Fisher, Alex, Amanda and Veronica exchanged a look as the implication of CURTIS's statement sunk in. Slowly, Amanda smiled and hopped off the windowsill.

"A couple of miles is walkable," she said. "So what are we waiting for?"

CHAPTER 9

NO TRESPASSING. VIOLATORS WILL BE MADE TO SORT 10,000 MOON ROCKS BY WEIGHT.

—SIGN SPOTTED ON M.O.R.O.N.S. FENCE

Exactly fifty-seven minutes later, Fisher, Alex, Amanda, and Veronica were staring out over the top of a low ridge. On the other side of the ridge was a flat expanse of long brown and tan grasses, lit up weakly with the last red rays of the setting sun. A chain-link fence made a giant square around a collection of dilapidated barns and grain silos. As darkness fell, Fisher popped open a pair of night vision binoculars that collapsed to the size of a postage stamp, and aimed them at a sign posted on the fence.

"'US Department of Agriculture Crop Testing Area,'" he read. "Nice. That's why there aren't a lot of guards around the perimeter. It would spoil the illusion."

"Here comes a patrol," said Amanda, pointing. "It looks like there are just two of them."

A pair of tan-clad guards rounded the far corner of the fence, passed only a dozen feet from them, and turned their backs at the near corner. The kids waited for more guards to pass as a cold wind whipped up the dust at their feet. An owl hooted somewhere in the trees, followed by a second. The chilly breeze kept up, and Fisher rubbed his hands together.

"Looks like it's just the one patrol," Veronica said, shivering.

"Okay then, let's move it," said Amanda. They crested the ridge and ran as quietly as they could down to the edge of the fence. Fisher removed a vial from his backpack as Alex and Amanda pulled on Fisher's strength sleeves—Alex had kept even more of them tucked away in his room. The dodgeball experience had given them a better idea how to use them. Fisher put a drop of his patented Screw Liquefier, which handily liquefied anything made of steel, at several key points in the fence. The fence began to drip like melting cheddar. Alex and Amanda pulled in opposite directions, opening a hole through which they all slipped.

When Alex and Amanda set the fence back in place, Fisher immediately reapplied the rapidly solidifying metal, and the fence was back to normal.

"Okay," Fisher said, looking over what appeared from the outside to be decrepit farm buildings, including several grain silos and an old barn. "So where's the ship?"

"I overheard Willard bragging about his dad and this

place to Brody," Amanda said. "I think the key point in this facility is the biggest silo." She pointed to a massive, round silo in the middle of the compound. "Let's take a look."

Ducking low, they ran toward the building's dark silhouette, scanning the landscape as they went. So far, they hadn't seen a single person other than the two guards.

Fisher was baffled. If there really *were* an extraterrestrial spacecraft concealed here, the place should be swarming with scientists and researchers. But the place was almost totally silent except for the occasional calls of the owls and the whispering wind. Could CURTIS have been wrong? Could this really be a place for agricultural crop testing after all?

"Down!" whispered Amanda harshly, pointing to the two guards in the distance.

They dropped as a group to the grass and Fisher took a thin, dark sheet from his pack, covering them with it. The sheet had a complex sensor system that quickly analyzed the colors and textures of the material around it. The sheet's material itself could then change its appearance accordingly. After a moment it turned a mottled green and black, and filmy blades of green sprang up from the tarp in imitation.

Fisher could only hear his own breathing for a few seconds, and then footsteps, growing louder. They had good camouflage, but it wouldn't do much good if they got stepped on.

The steps got closer. Twenty feet, ten, five. A boot came down two inches from Fisher's right ear, and he tensed every muscle in his body to keep from springing up and running.

The guards passed. Fisher waited another minute before throwing off the tarp and gesturing to his friends to move on.

The grain silo's wall was solid steel all the way around. No doors, no buttons—no way to enter at all.

"What now?" said Alex.

"Brody didn't believe Willard," Amanda said. "Willard demonstrated the password to back up his case. Let's see if he was telling the truth." She sighed, cleared her throat, and started whistling. The melody was weirdly familiar. Still, it took Fisher a minute to identify the melody.

"Is that . . . is that the tune to 'Gift-Wrapped Heart'?" Fisher said, flabbergasted.

"Yep, that's it," Veronica muttered. Even in the dark, it was obvious that she was blushing.

Pop sensation Kevin Keels had written "Gift-Wrapped Heart" back before he had been revealed as a tone-deaf lip-syncher, but maybe NASA was a little behind the times. The song had saved them once before, when it turned out Keels's real singing voice could literally kill robots.

What had been a featureless stretch of wall became a door, sliding open with a faint hiss. Inside was a small chamber of plain-brushed steel.

Amanda, Fisher, Alex, and Veronica passed inside together. The door shut behind them, dim bluish light glowed to life, and the little room, which turned out to be an elevator, began to descend.

The ride lasted for what felt like a *very* long time. When it finally began to slow, Alex muttered a warning.

"Be ready to fight," he said. "We don't know what's waiting for us on the other side of that door."

The elevator finally came to a halt, and the door hissed open, revealing . . . nothing.

"Fisher," Amanda whispered. "Where are we?"

"What *is* this?" Veronica added.

Beyond the door was pitch-darkness and heavy silence. It was like the elevator had taken them to the end of the universe. The bright light spilling from inside the elevator didn't even reflect onto the floor.

"I—I don't know," Fisher said. "It must be the weirdest security measure I've ever seen."

He took a deep breath and inched cautiously out of the elevator, hoping he would encounter solid ground and not a thousand-foot drop into nothingness. Instantly, the room burst into multicolored light. At the same moment, music began to play.

It was "Gift-Wrapped Heart."

"What the . . . ?" Amanda turned a full circle. The walls were bursting with kaleidoscopic colors. The floor was a pulsing white, and multiple colored trails moved across it in different directions. Fisher looked more closely. Each trail looked like footprints.

"Are these . . . dance instructions?" he said, looking at the shifting footprint patterns.

"Yes," Veronica said, cheeks bright red. "But only one of them is correct for this song. Please," she sighed and her face glowed even brighter, "allow me."

Fisher stepped aside. Veronica carefully followed the orange trail, stepping in time to the music, even miming with her arms. She kept going until the song reached its first chorus, and then everything but a simple soft light clicked off. Now the room just looked like a room, and a door was visible on the other side of it.

"Wow," Alex said. "I've never seen a *dance* lock before."

"I guess my Kevin Keels obsession had a bright side after all," Veronica panted, pushing a stray bit of hair out of her eyes.

The door slid open with a satisfying click. On the other side was a man-made cavern bigger than a basketball arena, crisscrossed by walkways and gantries holding immense machines. The sides of the excavated cave were studded with windows, probably offices, laboratories, and

Correct Sequence of Dance Steps
GIFT-WRAPPED HEART

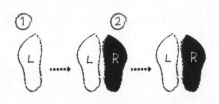

(silver ribbon)

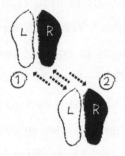

(in a tiny bow)

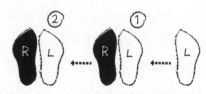

(untie it, baby)

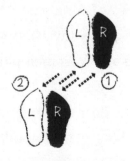

(but untie it slow)

REPEAT

living quarters. The floor far below them bustled with engineers and researchers.

And in the center of it was the Gemini's ship.

Fisher could tell it was designed to fly in atmosphere. It had a rounded, aerodynamic nose and a streamlined body with stubby wing-like extensions on either side. It was a dull turquoise color slashed with glinting black stripes, and had no visible engines.

There was a staircase down to their right and a door to their left.

Amanda started moving toward the stairs, but Alex grabbed the back of her shirt.

"If we take the stairs, we'll be spotted," said Alex, pointing to a series of cameras on the walkways, all of which were aimed down.

"Agreed," said Veronica. "Our best bet is the door. We can try to work our way down through the offices. There must be a secondary way down to the floor."

Fisher nodded and took the lead, the others forming up behind him like the well-trained team they had become. Fisher leaned against the door. In his left ear he inserted a mini-stethoscope the size of an earplug. He didn't hear anyone moving or speaking. He hoped that meant it was empty.

He opened the door and the others snuck in. Fisher closed it silently behind him. The room looked like a guard barracks, with two rows of bunks, a few posters on the walls, and a computer terminal on the cave-side wall underneath its broad window. There was also a promising-looking hatch in the floor, and a door on the far side of the room.

Amanda crossed to the second door, leaned in to listen, and then shook her head. "Footsteps. Coming this way, fast."

"We have to backtrack," said Alex, waving Fisher toward him. Fisher put his ear to the door they'd just come through. More footsteps.

"They're coming the other way, too," Fisher said, his breathing harsh in his own ears.

With no other choice, Veronica opened the floor hatch. It was a dark, ladderless tunnel.

"Down the hatch then," Veronica said as she hopped in. Alex threw a look at each door and followed her.

"After you," Fisher said, and Amanda jumped.

Fisher heard a door handle turn. He sat down at the edge of the hole in the floor, looked at the abyss into which his friends had vanished, and pulled the hatch closed after him as he followed them down.

For six seconds there was nothing but the *whoosh* of air rushing around his head. It must have been some kind of rapid deployment tunnel, for when guards were needed on the cave floor as quickly as possible. He hoped that meant that the landing would be soft—otherwise they'd splatter like pancake batter on a hot griddle.

After the sixth second, he felt air open around him for an instant, then the soft embrace of a flexible net. It was an immersion cloth of some kind, built to absorb momentum and cushion landings. It even had a fresh, linen-ish scent.

In fact, the cloth's components felt an awful lot like boxer shorts.

Fisher felt around some more and realized that the "net" he had landed in was a pile of underwear. They had gone down the laundry chute.

He dug himself out of the underwear as the others pulled the mercifully clean laundry off of themselves.

"Well, we're down," said Alex, removing a tank top from his forehead. "Let's go find that ship."

The laundry room led to a corridor. They moved carefully down the narrow hall. Suddenly, Alex held out an arm, stopping them in place. He pointed to a swiveling camera in the ceiling.

"My turn," said Alex, reaching into his pack. He withdrew a small tube, pointed it at the camera, and pressed a button. An almost invisible object zipped out and covered the camera's lens.

"I can make that membrane over the camera turn opaque, and then clear again, with the push of a button.

If I darken it for just a second or two, it'll just look like a momentary glitch. Everybody ready to run?" They all nodded.

Alex led the way, and they ran around the corner as Alex pressed a second button on the tube, releasing it the moment they passed out of the camera's view. They came to the mouth of the corridor and ducked behind a pile of supply crates.

The open cavern floor was ahead of them. No more than fifty feet away was the ship. It glimmered in the dim lighting of the lab, majestic and sleek.

Fisher noticed another figure, shrouded in shadow, searching through one of the supply crates. His blood turned to chunks of ice.

"Alex," Fisher whispered, gripping his clone's arm. From the way Alex stiffened, Fisher knew that he'd seen.

They would know that slender, sharp-faced profile anywhere. When the figure turned enough to throw light on its face, their worst fear was confirmed.

Dr. X.

CHAPTER 10

If you don't want to hide in the dark all the time, you have to get used to your shadow. *Even if your shadow is a crazy little man who wants to rule the world.*
                                    —Fisher Bas, Personal Notes

"He must be trying to steal the Gemini ship," Alex hissed.

"Come on," Fisher said. "We *have* to stop him."

The four kids lunged out of their hiding spot toward Dr. X, who spun on his heel just in time to see the leaping figures of Alex and Amanda. Amanda locked her arms around his ankles and Alex tackled him around the waist, bringing him down with a *whoomph*.

"Get him on his feet," Fisher said coldly.

Dr. X was, apart from Three, the most evil and dangerous human in the world.

Amanda and Alex hauled Dr. X up, and Amanda locked his arms behind his back. Veronica stood beside Fisher, her fists clenched in contempt.

"My dear, dear boy," X drawled, his smirk only increasing when Amanda squeezed his arms a little tighter. "Wherever our paths may take us, they seem ever to lead us back to each other. Perhaps that says something about us, don't you think?"

"Don't start your 'You're just like me' speech again," Fisher said, glowering. Dr. X and Fisher had been briefly allied in the fight against Three. But Dr. X had turned on Fisher in the end, and Fisher had regained control only when he had refused to partner with Dr. X permanently. "The last time you counted on me to act like you, it didn't turn out so well, did it?"

Dr. X's sly smile disintegrated.

"You wasted a perfect opportunity," spat Dr. X. "You have much to learn yet. But that doesn't make us opposites."

"Enough," Fisher said. "Enough of this. I'm going to turn you in."

Dr. X let out an amused laugh.

"Turn me in?" he said. "You seem to have mistaken which one of us is the criminal party here."

Dr. X looked pointedly at Fisher's torso. Fisher looked down and realized he was covered in red laser dots. So were Veronica, Amanda, and Alex.

Fisher turned around slowly. Armored guards surrounded them, and Fisher recognized many of the same men who had been on patrol at Loopity Land. They were everywhere—crouched behind crates and equipment, peeking out from every shadowed corner.

"Hands up," one of them bellowed. Fisher, Alex, and

Veronica raised their hands in the air. Reluctantly, so did Amanda, though it meant releasing Dr. X.

One of the guards came forward, and Fisher recognized him as the sergeant who'd commanded the Loopity Land team.

"Stand down," the man said, with a hand on his headset, and the dots winked out. "Were you harmed?" He directed the question at Dr. X.

"Whoa, whoa, hold on," Fisher said, trying to hide his anger and astonishment. The security guard was treating Dr. X as his top priority. "Sergeant, I think you've been misled. This man is—"

"Harold Granger, alias Dr. Xander, commonly known as Dr. X," said the sergeant. "We know exactly who he is and what he's done. Believe me, I'd like nothing more than to Velcro him to a wall and use him for penalty kick practice. But my orders say otherwise. Now then, Doctor, is everything all right?"

"Fine, just fine," said Dr. X, smiling again and dusting off his immaculate white lab coat. "A simple misunderstanding between old friends—it happens all the time. In fact, with your permission, I actually think these four could be very *useful* to my work."

Fisher's jaw dropped open so wide, it could've accommodated a 747. Was Dr. X, international criminal, evil genius, attempted world conqueror, giving *them* permission to stay? Was he asking for their *help*?

The sergeant looked from Fisher to Veronica to Alex to Amanda, then nodded.

"As you say, sir," he said. "And I'd rather not let it get out that a pack of kids got past my security."

"I wish I could see this guy twirling around to Kevin Keels," Alex whispered.

The sergeant turned toward the kids, his mouth a thin line. "If the doc says you can help, you can help. Oh, I have something for you Bas boys," he said, handing Fisher a small piece of paper.

Alex leaned in to look.

Dear boys, began the note in their mother's handwriting, *we're going to be in Washington a while longer. We had a feeling you would seek out the Gemini ship. If you do, don't be alarmed by Dr. X. The government decided to let him fill in for us. We don't like it, but in this situation we don't think there's much choice. Hope to see you soon! XO, Mom*

"Huh," Alex said. "As weird as it sounds, sometimes I forget how smart they are."

On the sergeant's signal, the guards melted into the background as quickly as they'd appeared, leaving Dr. X and the kids alone in front of the Gemini spacecraft, although Fisher had no doubt they were being observed.

"You're *working* for them?" Amanda blurted out as Dr.

X booted up a massive computer terminal sitting next to the ship.

"In a situation like this, the government needs the best available," said Dr. X. "And I *am* the best."

A chill shot straight through Fisher. Dr. X's words, and the sergeant's attitude, confirmed his worst suspicions. The aliens were a threat—and they needed to be stopped.

"Exactly . . . what *is* our situation?" said Fisher.

The screen on the computer flickered on, showing a star chart with a connect-the-dots line jumping from star to star over a path several hundred light-years long.

"It's taken a massive amount of computing power, but we've been able to translate the digital language of this ship's computer," said Dr. X. "We can only access a little bit at a time, so we cracked navigation first. This chart shows the path the Gemini have been traveling for the past two hundred years."

"Two *centuries*?" said Amanda.

"There's no telling how long the Gemini's lifespan is," said Alex. "For all we know, it could be centuries, millennia."

According to the charts, the Gemini had been very busy planet-hopping in those two hundred years. Fisher recognized the star where the path ended as the Sun— only the latest in a very long string of stops.

"They've come such a long way," he said. "Barely

stopping long enough to leave a mark. Maybe they're running away from something."

"Frankly," Dr. X said, "if the Gemini creature is running from anything, it's the ruin caused by its own appetites. The being you named the Gemini has adopted a nomadic existence. It travels from planet to planet, resides there for a number of years, and then moves on. Based on our observations of its behavior, I can only conclude that it strips each planet of whatever resources it possesses, growing to an immense size in the process. It would likely churn out more and more of its drones to collect resources and support this growth, creating the illusion of a 'population.' As the resources begin to dwindle, the entity begins to shrink, until it finally re-embarks on this ship to move on to the next world. Basically, it is an extremely adaptive space parasite."

Veronica's expression was grim. Fisher knew exactly what she was imagining: the Earth reduced to a barren desert, all life extinct, oceans drained, the soil itself consumed, stripped to the bedrock.

It was all his fault. He'd launched the M3. He'd welcomed the Gemini to Earth with open arms. He'd made every effort to be friendly and accommodating. Had he just been ringing a dinner bell, and were the students of Wompalog served as the appetizer?

Of all the mistakes he'd made in his life, this one was

most certainly the worst. And the way this school year had gone, that was truly saying something.

He had to fix it.

"In the chaos of the crash landing and the explosion of the M3, we were able to retrieve their ship," Dr. X said. "Our teams dug it out of the debris as quickly as possible and got it back here hidden in a flatbed truck disguised as a wreckage hauler. We haven't yet been able to access the interior, but we've scanned it."

A graphic chart popped up, showing various rooms and corridors within the ship, slightly bigger than human-sized ones would be.

"Wait a minute," said Fisher, hoping to catch a flaw in Dr. X's calculations. "In its natural state the Gemini is a puddle of liquid. It can take any solid form it wants. Why would it build a ship full of big rooms and hallways? That's a highly inefficient use of space. Unless . . . " His throat tightened up.

"Unless it did *not* build this ship," said Dr. X with a thin smile.

Amanda groaned. "Don't tell me," she said. "More aliens?"

Dr. X inclined his head. "My conclusion exactly."

Amanda and Veronica stared at each other, horrified.

"So the Gemini hijacked this ship," Amanda said. "And, I'm guessing, ate its crew."

GEMINI SHIP

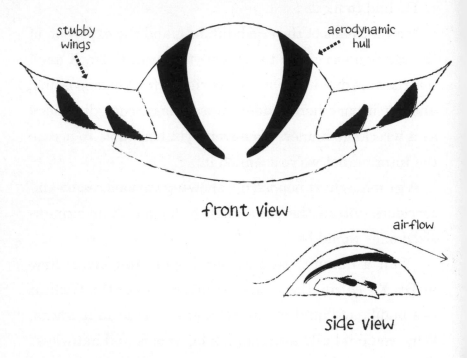

stubby wings

aerodynamic hull

front view

airflow

side view

Dr. X flicked the star chart to the side with a touch, replacing it with an animation displaying the story Dr. X went on to tell.

"It's my theory that the Gemini existed for millions of years on its native planet, its growth controlled and balanced by natural predators." The screen showed a globe, with a fluctuating green area representing the Gemini growing and shrinking, harmonious with its environment. "Then an alien ship, explorers probably, touched down."

A close-up view showed the ship descending to the surface. Stick figures emerged after touchdown. A green puddle approached the ship, and gradually the puddle turned into identical stick figures.

"With the Gemini's amazing ability to change shape, it mimicked the crew of the ship, infiltrating, eliminating, and replacing them." The original stick figures vanished and the Gemini copies walked onto the ship.

"Eliminating and *eating*," Amanda stressed.

"So," Veronica said, "they're like a locust swarm. Sweeping across the galaxy, devouring whatever they find. And they'll keep eating until there's nothing left. A group of ill-fated astronauts from somewhere in space set this whole cycle in motion two centuries ago. With no natural predators on the other planets it hit, it just kept growing until it had eaten everything, and was forced to move on." No one contradicted her and she shivered. "I wonder how many civilizations have turned to dust in its path."

"Well, that's the one bit of good news," said Dr. X. "Based on our best estimates of the distribution of life in the galaxy, Earth is probably the first planet the Gemini has hit that's home to an intelligent and technologically advanced species. That's why it spent so much time studying us before landing."

"Which means this is the first chance to stop them,"

said Fisher. The whole situation had turned around in his head. He'd thought, hoped, that the Gemini would bring wisdom and technology, enlightenment and insight, to Earth.

Instead, all they'd brought was an appetite.

CHAPTER 11

It wasn't until I met aliens who acted like humans that I truly understood how annoying humans are.
—Amanda Cantrell, Diary

"This may be the single biggest danger humanity's ever faced. But how come they brought *you* in?" said Alex, frowning darkly up at Dr. X.

"Yeah," said Fisher. "As I recall, you were supposed to be spending the next few lifetimes in a little concrete room eating canned string beans off of a Styrofoam tray. Besides, you've tried to rule the world twice. Why would you even *want* to help?"

"My boy," Dr. X said, "exactly how much of a world would be left for me to rule after the Gemini have consumed it? I am as invested in our planet's survival as you are. I was temporarily released from my prison because, like it or not, my country—my world—*needs* my help. Besides"—he lifted his arm, allowing the sleeve of his white coat to fall down and revealing a tight steel bracelet—"I'm on a very, very short leash. A leash that will render me unconscious if I pull on it too hard," he said.

Fisher and Alex exchanged a look. At least Dr. X was

being very closely monitored. Clearly, the MORONS weren't taking any chances.

"All right," Fisher said, sighing. "So what else do you know?"

"Fortunately, I've been able to make significant repairs to this craft," Dr. X said, pointing up at the prow of the ship jutting high overhead. The metal glimmered in the lab lights. "But there is still an enormous quantity of work to do. I could use your help," he added bluntly.

"What kind of help?" said Amanda, narrowing her eyes.

"There are some . . . items I need you to fetch for me," Dr. X said. For the first time, he seemed uncomfortable. He wouldn't look Fisher in the eye, but instead studied the hull of the ship, as if the most fascinating story ever were written there.

Warning lights started blinking in Fisher's mind. Dr. X was a genius, and he could plan very far ahead. He might continue asking for seemingly harmless items for days or weeks, all the while assembling them into some kind of weapon for his escape.

"What kind of items?" Alex said coldly. He was obviously thinking the same thing as Fisher was.

"The food here is terrible," said Dr. X with a shrug. "I'd like, for starters, a truly gargantuan Reuben sandwich."

"You want us to make a deli run??" Amanda squealed,

outraged. "When the future of our species is at stake?"

"How do you expect me to save our world with an unsatisfied gullet?" X said, blinking at her. "And perhaps on Thursday a turkey might not be out of the question. It is Thanksgiving, after all."

Fisher looked at Alex.

"Is there anything non-food related on your list?" Fisher said. "Anything at all?"

"Possibly," Dr. X said. He turned back to the chart of the ship projected on his computer. "See here? There's a large cavity in the ship's port side. It looks like a cargo chamber—but missing its cargo. We've had teams scouring the crash site, but saw no evidence of damaged freight. Any ideas?"

Fisher puzzled over the diagram.

"I don't know," he said, scratching his chin. "Maybe it's some kind of escape pod? Maybe the Gemini loaded and jettisoned important equipment so it wouldn't be hurt in the crash?"

"Could be," agreed Alex. "Or maybe it was a backup power source or a secondary engine."

"We've barely been able to restore minimal power to this ship," Dr. X said. "If the missing item is a fully functional piece of this ship's technology, then studying it in operation would give us very valuable information. Perhaps you might be able to locate it, particularly since you

Gemini Trajectory
Through Space

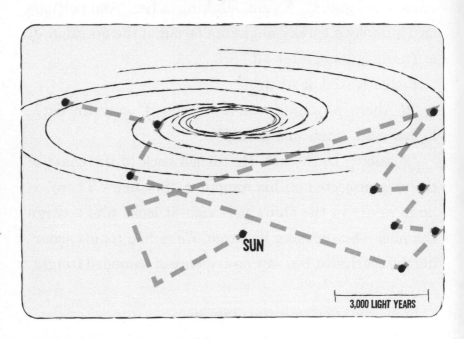

3,000 LIGHT YEARS

have an in with the Gemini."

"Yeah, about that." Alex coughed. "I think relations are a little sour at the moment."

"Still, we have to try," Fisher said. Despite his hatred of the evil former teacher/megalomaniac, Dr. X did have a good point. "If we can figure out their technology, we might be able to get in the ship and use it to our advantage. The Gemini must have a weakness. We just need to figure out what it is."

"Agreed," said Veronica. "It's time to reclaim the Earth."

"Absolutely!" Dr. X said. He turned to Fisher and put his hand up. "High five!"

Fisher sent a crinkled look at Alex, but after a moment's pause he slapped his own palm into Dr. X's, hopefully hard enough to sting.

"It's settled, then," said Dr. X. "Find the missing mystery piece of the ship, study it in operation, and bring me as much data as possible. And don't forget that sandwich—extra sauerkraut."

≋ CHAPTER 12 ≋

Maybe our next space mission should be to put a giant "closed for repairs" sign in orbit around Earth.

—Alex Bas, Personal Notes

An official car whisked them home from the lab, dropping first Veronica and then Amanda off at home. Once they were alone, Alex turned to Fisher, his eyes gleaming in the dark.

"I think I know a way to earn the Gemini's trust back," he said.

Fisher felt a pulse of apprehension. He was still not entirely over the days when most of Alex's plans had involved explosive materials and/or detention. "Go on," he said.

"Well," Alex's mouth quirked into a smile. "The Gemini like *parties*, don't they?"

"Yep," Fisher said, sighing. "Almost as much as they love eating."

"Exactly," Alex said as the car pulled up to the curb. "Seems to me they'd really enjoy a national party about eating, don't you think?"

Fisher's thoughts snapped right into line with his clone's.

"I think I see where you're going with this," he said, stepping out of the car.

Taking a deep breath, Fisher approached the silver, bullet-like bus parked curbside by the Bas house, Alex a step behind him. Alex's plan was simple but brilliant. Inviting the Gemini to join in the Thanksgiving celebrations would surely convince them that the humans meant them no harm. Maybe then he might even *ask* about the missing piece from the ship. But whatever he did, he had to be sure they didn't suspect that their ship was in Dr. X's claw-like hands.

He reached up a hand to knock, but before he could, the door swung open, revealing Anna and Bee, hands planted on hips, green eyes shining ominously.

"H-hello," he said in as cheerful a tone he could muster toward beings who intended to eat his home planet. "We, um, we realize that we've had some troubles communicating. As the Earth representative, I'm here to propose a solution. Can I come in?"

Anna and Bee hesitated for only a second before moving aside. As Fisher and Alex climbed up into the bus, he tried not to think about the fact that they weren't two separate girls, but actually two random appendages of an enormous, goop-like alien creature.

He smiled nervously. The bus was packed with Gemini. They fell silent when they saw the boys. Fisher cleared his throat.

"This week, people in our part of the world have a

celebration called Thanksgiving," Alex said. "It commemorates the meeting of two different civilizations, and celebrates a moment in time when they worked together in peace."

"Yes," said Anna, "we learned about Thanksgiving when we were studying you." She wasn't smiling.

"Good!" Fisher squeaked. He was sweating. Was it his imagination, or did the Gemini look . . . hungry? "Then you must have seen the big parade that happens in New York City," he rushed on quickly. "It just so happens that we've got our own Thanksgiving parade at Wompalog. It's a big school tradition. It takes place on the Tuesday before Thanksgiving, which is tomorrow. Short notice, I know, but we'd like you to participate." When Anna looked unmoved, he added, "There will be balloons and floats and . . . and . . . costumes!"

The word *costumes* obviously had the desired effect. There was another fractional moment of hesitation, and Fisher had the weirdest sensation that the Gemini were communicating soundlessly, all together, the way muscles communicate, or cells.

Anna smiled at last. "Thank you for the invitation. We would be thrilled to participate."

"Wonderful," Fisher said, trying to smile but managing only to grimace. Already, he was imagining Terence the Towering Turkey going up in a cloud of scorched feathers and papier-mâché smoke.

"In fact, we have just the thing for a *float*, as you call it," Anna said calmly. "We will use our small shuttlecraft. It will look very pretty decorated with balloons."

"Shuttlecraft?" Fisher said, trying to mask the surprise in his voice. With hardly any effort, he'd learned that Dr. X's assumption was correct: an important part of the ship *was* missing.

"Yes," Bee said. She didn't seem to notice Fisher's sudden interest. "It's waiting for us in orbit and can be called down at any time. We will—what's the word?—camouflage it so that it is suitable for your parade."

Fisher had to bite his lip to keep from shouting for joy. It was almost *too* easy. He'd thought he'd have to tease clues about the object's whereabouts from the Gemini over the course of days, and then track it down himself. Instead, the Gemini were going to practically drop the shuttlecraft at his feet.

"That would be perfect," Fisher said, smiling. And for the first time in a long time, he thought that maybe the humans had a shot against the Gemini after all.

≋ CHAPTER 13 ≋

*I thought sprinkling salt on me was a local greeting custom.
Then they turned on the oven.*
    —Hal Torque, brief sidekick to Vic Daring, Issue #122

"These feathers are stabbing me in the back," said Alex, shifting his position.

"Funny, you could say the same thing about the Gemini," said Fisher drily.

It was Tuesday afternoon, and the Wompalog Thanksgiving Parade was about to begin. Everyone had the morning off from school for the celebration. Fisher and Alex stood on top of Terence the Towering Turkey, the biggest and most beloved float, usually the last in the procession. The monstrous bird had papier-mâché feathers in every color imaginable and his beak was the product of one of the earliest ceramics projects in the art department's history. As was the custom, the float would be towed by Principal Teed in his car.

Their parents still hadn't returned from Washington. Another message had been sent to them through the sergeant of the guard. Apparently Mr. and Mrs. Bas were making progress, but they weren't sure how much longer they would be. Fisher was starting to wonder if Palo Alto would still be around when they got back. Making sure this parade went smoothly would be a crucial step to ensure it would.

The Wompalog Thanksgiving Day Parade had started by accident. Many years ago, the Wompalog cafeteria had been preparing to serve a special Thanksgiving lunch on the Tuesday before the holiday, and a group of eighth graders plotted to steal the turkey. They slipped into the cafeteria, grabbed the big cart that the huge roast turkey was sitting on, and rolled it right out of the school and down the street. Cafeteria staff chased after them, followed by other kids who'd heard the commotion. The following year a group of kids commemorated the event by creating Terence and rolling him down the street to cheers from the whole school.

But by now, the parade was a true Wompalog tradition.

The school's trailers had been cleared to the far side of the King of Hollywood parking lot, creating a vast space in which the various floats could congregate before setting off. Wompalog Middle School was abuzz with the news that the girls from Geminolvia were going to take part in the Thanksgiving parade, and Teed expected record attendees—all of which made Fisher very, very nervous.

Fisher adjusted his position against the turkey's neck. They would have to be incredibly careful. Somehow,

Fisher didn't think the Gemini would react well if they knew that the humans were taking such an interest in their shuttlecraft.

That's why Fisher, Alex, Amanda, and Veronica were camouflaged in experimental suits. Fisher had spent a sleepless night analyzing a tiny sample of Gemini residue. With the resources available at the MORONS laboratory, mini-generators, and the—much as it made his stomach churn to admit it—help of Dr. X, he'd redesigned his old spy suits with the ability to automatically change their appearance and shape to match their surroundings. It even included a manual mode that let the wearer choose the suit's shape, regardless of the environment. Fisher called them ChameleoClothes.

At the moment, the ChameleoClothes were manifesting itchypaper feathers that smelled vaguely like decade-old cheese.

"Keep your eyes open," Fisher whispered, awkwardly shifting the bulk of the suit as he reached up and planted a miniature radar dish on the underside of Terence's beak. He affixed it with quick-drying glue. Fisher looked down at a screen attached to his wrist and a field of blips and fuzzy shapes popped up. He would be able to keep track of all activity in and around the parade.

In Alex's backpack was the portable scanner entrusted to him by Dr. X. If they could attach it to the hull of the

Gemini shuttle for just thirty seconds, it would reveal and store details of the shuttlecraft's interior *and* exterior. With this knowledge, they could finish repairing the big ship and even unlock its main hatch.

Fisher raised a hand to his ear and tapped the nearly invisible earbud he was wearing.

"Amanda, are you and Veronica in place? Over."

"Copy, in position on the condiments float. Feeling ridiculous."

"You're supposed to say 'over.' Over."

"Are you serious? Fine, *over*."

Fisher could feel Amanda's annoyance through the earbud. He held up a pair of binoculars and shaded the lens from the bright California sun. The binoculars autofocused until the girls were in sight.

Amanda and Veronica were across the parking lot on one of the very first floats. Their suits were bright red and bumpy to help them blend into the huge bowl of foam cranberry sauce they were hiding in. Amanda and Veronica would create a diversion by using the condiments float's famous Cran-Cannons. At the end of the parade route there were several targets set up, and a part of the big finale was a marksmanship contest wherein several lucky volunteers would try to launch massive globs of cranberry sauce with great accuracy. If Amanda and Veronica could get to those cannons, that might distract

Schematics for
CHAMELEOCLOTHES

FRONT

BACK

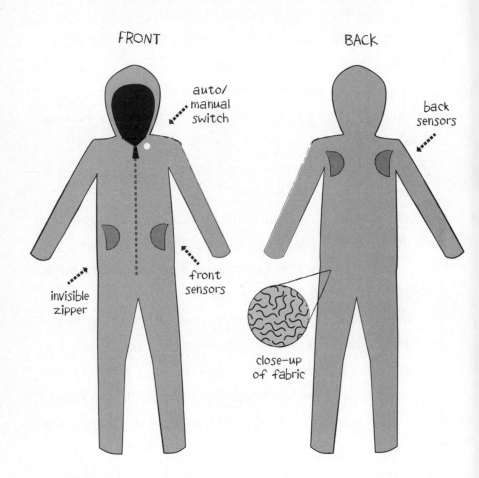

auto/
manual
switch

back
sensors

invisible
zipper

front
sensors

close-up
of fabric

the Gemini long enough for Fisher and Alex to approach
and scan the shuttle.

"Now we just have to wait for the aliens to show,"
Alex sighed.

No sooner had he said it than a low hum filled the lot, making their ears buzz and sending flurries of dust and pebbles skittering along the vibrating asphalt.

"Here we go," Fisher said, tapping his earpiece. "Stay hidden until we're ready to launch the diversion. Over."

"Got it," Amanda responded. *"Over,"* she added in an annoyed voice before Fisher could remind her.

Cheers from the onlookers pealed across the lot as the disguised Gemini shuttle appeared. Fisher had to admit it looked amazing. It floated gracefully out into the open, seeming to glide on the air—which, Fisher knew, was exactly what it was doing, though it was draped with a cloth to conceal the fact that it didn't have wheels. It was covered in balloons and swirls of fabric painted in browns, reds, and golds, and the back sprouted a turkey tail-like crest of construction paper feathers. And as it rotated slightly from left to right, the gleam of thousands of tiny sparkles dazzled the crowd.

Eight of the Gemini, including Anna and Bee, were standing on a platform built on top of the craft. They waved and smiled. *Lulling the population into blissful unawareness,* Fisher thought to himself.

Principal Teed wiggled out of the sunroof of his car, holding a bullhorn.

"Welcome one and all, particularly our new friends"—cheers broke out again—"to the forty-eighth annual

Wompalog Middle School Thanksgiving Parade!" Thunderous applause echoed throughout the parking lot.

Principal Teed disappeared once again into his car and honked the horn, signaling the parade could begin.

The first float was a display of a field of maize accented by squash and pumpkins on sticks, complete with waving scarecrows. The maize looked like it had been sitting in the sun for a few too many years without being harvested, but the float was neatly put together and did a good job setting the tone. The second float was a reasonably authentic miniature version of a Native American longhouse, upon which stood eighth grader Grace Beaumont, who was half Iroquois. After that was the float full of side dishes where Veronica and Amanda were hunkered down.

The parade slowly unspooled from a clump in the parking lot to its full length along the street. Hundreds of people were clustered behind the sidewalk barricades shouting and waving. Teed had been right. The crowd was even bigger than usual. Fisher swallowed hard. Nothing bad would happen. Nothing bad *could* happen.

Ahead of the Gemini shuttle was a marching band from a nearby high school. The trombones were a little warbly, but the sound was solid overall.

Fisher looked down to check the radar and it was right on target, the dots and clumps moving just as they should be.

"Hey, Fisher," Alex said, "how many snare drummers are in that band?"

"I didn't count," Fisher said. "Four, maybe?"

"That's what I thought," Alex said. "There are eight now."

Fisher looked up from the radar screen, his heart ramping up to panic speed. Eight snare drummers marched in the band. Four of them were real. The other four had to be Gemini, using their powers of transformation to disrupt the parade. After a moment, Fisher saw which were the impostors: four of them abruptly changed tempo, speeding their beat up to double time. About half the band tried to follow their rhythm, marching at double the speed of the rest of the band. Ringing crashes rang out as trumpets smacked into tubas, tall hats were swiped off by trombone slides, and bass drums scooped up everything in their path.

Spectators stumbled backward as musicians lurched, tripped, and floundered, crashing into the barricades that kept the spectators from spilling into the street.

"Is there a techno remix happening back there, or did something go wrong? Over," said Amanda over the radio.

"Wrong," Fisher said.

"I'm wrong? You forgot to say *over.*"

"No, right. I mean, something went wrong," Fisher responded, getting flustered. "The Gemini are disguising themselves as drummers and messing up the whole parade rhythm. We'll try to sort it out. Over."

Floats were starting and then jerking to a stop. The band itself was a few measures away from being a brass heap. The crowd, at least, was amused. They laughed and pointed as people in costumes stopped abruptly and collided with one another, as the tempo changed frenetically every few bars.

It was chaos. The mission had changed.

"Come on!" Fisher said, jumping off of the float and hitting the ground hard. Alex followed him. They both tapped buttons on their suit collars, switching the ChameleoClothes from "auto" to "manual." A few more taps later, Fisher's disguise immediately puffed out and turned the golden brown of corn bread while Alex's shifted to the many-hued cobble pattern of an ear of maize.

Fisher pulled two small boxes from his backpack, and tossed one to Alex. Moving as quickly as they could in the cumbersome costumes, they ran to opposite sides of the street, ducking around the colliding band members.

Fisher had brought the devices to help time and coordinate the group's efforts more exactly—but they were going to have to serve a different purpose now. He pressed a switch on his device, a speaker he'd been working on to help develop his dancing skills before he'd perfected the technology in the iGotRhythm automated dancing shoe. The speakers pumped out an extremely powerful beat at subsonic frequencies; a beat too low to hear, but powerful enough to *feel* all through the skeleton. Fisher adjusted the tempo to match that of the real drummers, and soon the rest of the band began to regain control, the inaudible *thud-thud* of the speakers too powerful to ignore.

By the time the band had resumed formation, the four impostor drummers were gone.

But Fisher couldn't relax. There could be Gemini *anywhere.* If the Gemini wanted to make trouble, he had no doubt they would. His eyes moved to the crowd. Was that old man's posture natural? Had he ever seen that girl around town before? Who would the Gemini most likely go after next?

Fisher jogged ahead to walk beside the colonial thatched-roof house float, hoping to get a better view.

"Hey, Fisher?" Amanda's voice patched in through his earbud. "The parade's supposed to go down Main Street this year, right?"

"Of course," Fisher said. "The same as every year."

"Well it isn't," Amanda said. "You'd better get up here. Um, over."

Fisher motioned for Alex to follow him. They ran past the plastic colonial house, past the side-dish float with its piles of cardboard stuffing and a few real giant corn ears that had survived poor Fee's fall in Mrs. Bas's garden. Panting, they finally reached the condiment float where

Amanda and Veronica were hiding. Amanda and Veronica hopped to the ground. Their suits morphed to look like twin green apple bushels, sprouting various leafy branches laden with fruit.

"Look," Veronica said, pointing. Up ahead, Main Street forked. A cop stood directing the parade along its intended route. His back was turned to an *identical* cop, who had moved the barricades and was directing the parade to bear left toward South Oak Street.

Fisher peered through his binoculars. The cops were *almost* identical. But the second cop's badge had no detail; it was solid and featureless. Also, his eyebrows looked like they'd been drawn on with Magic Marker. The cop was a Gemini decoy—badly made, hastily drawn.

The longhouse float had already turned left. The condiments float came to an abrupt halt at the fork, swaying, its driver apparently unsure which way to go.

"You go take that cop down," Fisher said to Amanda and Alex. "We'll run ahead and try to reroute the longhouse."

Fisher and Veronica bolted down the street, sending halfhearted waves to the parade watchers so that no one would be alarmed. Fisher fought down a surge of frustration. If the Gemini kept making trouble, Fisher and Alex would have to spend all their time preventing disaster and they wouldn't ever get close to the shuttle. He couldn't help wondering if the Gemini knew somehow, if they'd anticipated Fisher and Alex might use the parade to regain a strategic advantage and were taking steps to prevent it.

They bolted past the fake cop. Fisher had full confidence that Alex and Amanda would be able to take him down. The longhouse float was cruising down South Oak Street, a route that hadn't been cleared of traffic for the parade. Fisher's heart flapped in his throat like a dying fish.

Coming directly toward the float was a flatbed truck loaded up with antique clocks and fine porcelain dishes.

"You have to be kidding me," Fisher gasped out, picking up his pace, his lungs and legs burning with the effort.

The truck swerved toward the sidewalk. But even with the float hauling to the right, they looked certain to clip each other. The float may only have been going fifteen miles an hour, but given its size and the truck's load of breakable cargo, it was more than enough for a heavy crash.

"Veronica!" Fisher rooted in his backpack with one hand and tossed her a slingshot and a small black pellet. "Hit the truck!"

Without asking any questions, Veronica stopped to take aim. The black projectile sailed over Fisher's head, landing in the truck's bed and bursting into a purple foam, a buoyant material that would protect and buffer the cargo from any shocks.

Fisher kept running and at last pulled up alongside the float. The truck was almost on top of them. He had only seconds to act. He took a magnetic clamp from his belt and slapped it to the steel undercarriage. Spooling an almost invisible thread from the clamp, he hooked it to a dart, and threw it at a lamppost as they glided past an intersection.

Fisher's wire wrapped around the base of the lamppost and caught. The nylon thread—actually made of an incredibly durable steel fiber patented by Fisher's mother—halted the float in its tracks and, slowly, guided it to the right.

The truck and the float just brushed each other as the truck blew by, pounding its horn. The cargo jostled heavily, but the extra padding kept it safe. Fisher pulled a special blade from his belt and severed the wire as the float completed its turn, rounding the corner and heading back toward Main Street. At the speed it was going, it should merge with the rest of the parade at just the right spot to slot back into its space.

Alex and Amanda caught up to Fisher and Veronica.

"We took down the cop drone," said Amanda.

"How?" Veronica asked.

"Made fun of its eyebrows," Amanda said. "Until it went *kaboom*."

Screams broke out from the parade route.

"Sounds like the party's not over," said Alex, who tore off along the side street that connected with the parade. Fisher, Amanda, and Veronica sprinted behind him.

Principal Teed had commandeered the condiments float, and was deploying the Cran-Cannons. Tart ammunition went in every direction, dousing the crowd. The principal's grin was a little bit *too* wide—and in the very back of the parade, the *real* Principal Teed was still sitting behind the wheel of his Volvo.

Fisher groaned.

"Okay," Amanda said. "Suggestions?"

"I have one," said Veronica, raising an eyebrow.

The condiment float kept up its berry bombardment, gallons of sauce flying every which way, as spectators screamed and scattered, coated in the thick, purple goo.

Fisher, Alex, Veronica, and Amanda came running at the float from four different directions. The condiment float was decorated with many food items, including a number of massive squash stuck on the sides. The kids each grabbed one. Together, they stuffed the barrels with the squashes—then ran, rolled, or leapt out of the way.

The cannons, powered by air pressure, were now completely stopped up. When the Gemini drone went to deploy the next round of cranberry ammunition, the cannons instead *backfired*. The center of the float burst open, dousing the drone in red berry sauce. The fake Principal

Teed, drenched in red, let out a frightening roar. He took two long strides and a running leap from the side of the float into the crowd.

Then he was simply gone. He had merged with the crowd of panicked onlookers instantly—maybe even shape-shifting as he went.

The thought gave Fisher the chills.

Fisher picked himself up from the ground. The crowd was still scattering, pushing and shoving to escape the cranberry barrage. The few remaining spectators were staring over Fisher's shoulder with horrified looks on their faces.

Fisher turned to see why and nearly froze solid himself.

The Gemini had taken on a new form.

Four giant turkeys were clomping down the street, the ground trembling beneath their massive claws.

≫ CHAPTER 14 ≪

You cannot hope to truly understand how an alien mind works. You can only hope it understands that you do not wish to be vaporized.

—*Vic Daring, Issue #235*

Each turkey was roughly the size of a sedan. The poultry moved together, quickly, black eyes gleaming with malice.

"It was only a matter of time," Amanda said. "The Gemini don't like it when their plans get messed up. We've made ourselves a threat, and they're coming after us."

"Fisher!" Alex cried. He had snatched the binoculars from Fisher's hand and was peering through them. "The Gemini's shuttle is completely unguarded. Now's our chance to get close!"

"Okay," Veronica said, taking a deep breath. "Alex, you and Amanda go get that scan done. Fisher and I will distract the turkeys."

Alex and Amanda dashed off toward the end of the parade, leaping over splintered police barricades and ducking through the dispersing crowd, giving the massive, lumbering turkeys a wide berth.

The Gemini were going all-out now. Fisher wasn't sure

why they were causing such havoc in the parade—what did they have to gain? But he had a feeling this was just a test. They were testing how people reacted to them. They were seeing how much they could get away with. The kids had interfered with their test, and now the Gemini were coming to get them out of the way. Alex and Amanda had escaped their notice for now, but they had Fisher and Veronica dead in their sights.

"We're at the shuttle," came Amanda's voice in Fisher's ear. "We need twenty seconds! Over!"

One turkey had zeroed in on Fisher. He sidestepped one way, then the other, before diving left, like an asteroid being yanked into a new path by Jupiter. The turkey lunged down, its beak pecking the street so hard it cracked. It missed Fisher by inches.

A scattering of applause rose up from the remaining crowd. Fisher realized that they must think this was *planned*—a kind of stage combat spectacular.

Veronica rolled under the legs of another as it swept toward her, coming up on her feet just in time to duck under a second one's head swipe.

"Fifteen. Over," Amanda said.

Fisher ran in circles around one mammoth bird as it aimed talon slashes at him. He jumped over one claw, hit the ground hard, and rolled underneath a second. Veronica jumped to the side as the two birds chasing her both lunged simultaneously. Their hive mind kept them from colliding, but the complex dodge they had to execute was enough to give Veronica a moment to breathe.

"Ten," Amanda said.

Two turkeys were bearing down on Fisher. He looked from one to the other rapidly, then made a dash and grabbed one's leg, wrapping himself around it. It kicked hard. Fisher felt like his insides were being rearranged, but he clung as tightly as he could and the bird couldn't dislodge him. The other one aimed a peck at him but only hit his side on the wing.

"Five," Amanda said.

Fisher clutched the turkey's leg for all he was worth. Veronica hit one of hers in the side of the foot, tripping it.

"Got it!" Amanda said.

"RUN!" Fisher bellowed. The turkey's next kick hurled him through the air and straight into the "feathery" embrace of the Terence the Towering Turkey float, which was still being driven by the real, and very confused, Principal Teed. Veronica sprinted full tilt between the four mega-turkeys, turning her suit to a dull black to lose them. The Gemini turkeys, having lost their prey, trotted back toward the shuttle, disappearing behind the network of vast floats still clogging the street. Seconds later, eight girls emerged, resuming their position at the top of their shuttle as though nothing had happened.

Big cheers went up from the crowd. Everyone had loved the show. Even though he was shaking, Fisher took a little bow, forcing a smile on his face, trying to maintain the impression that this had all been planned.

The parade limped to its end, dinged, and mostly covered in cranberry sauce but still intact. The bewildered kids on the floats looked exhausted, and the marching band had long ago stopped playing. Little bits of float decorations lay scattered along the route like battlefield wreckage. Which it basically was.

Fisher took another look around to make sure the floats were all accounted for. They all were, save one. The shuttle, and the Gemini, had disappeared.

CHAPTER 15

I never thought I'd say this, but I miss fighting robot dinosaurs.

—Fisher Bas, Personal Notes

"We got a complete scan," Alex said, sliding the device into his pack. "Let's hope this is all we need to get the Gemini ship up and running again."

"Let's pray," Fisher said, brushing a few red specks of cranberry from his sleeve. "They've changed their tactics. They're not interested in sneaking around anymore. They're causing chaos, panic. We've got to get them off Earth before things get any worse and they begin to cause real damage. I think the parade was them flexing their muscle a little to see if anyone caught on to what they really are. Nobody did. What few people stuck around till the end of the parade were too busy cleaning up to even notice they'd gone."

"I agree, that was probably just a test," Veronica said. "To see how much they can get away with. Unfortunately"—her blue eyes flashed a stormy color—"it looks like they can get away with quite a lot."

"They're moving to another phase of their plan," Alex said darkly.

"We need backup," Amanda said.

"We need Mason," Fisher said. "I can't believe he hasn't shown up."

"He didn't answer last night," Alex said. "And he hasn't returned my message."

Fisher and Alex scowled at the ground, which their basically identical appearance made sort of comical.

"That's not like him," Fisher said, feeling a little dejected. Agent Mason always came through for them when they were in a pinch. Didn't he realize that they wouldn't call unless it was an emergency? "The fate of humanity is at stake and he isn't even in his office?"

Veronica laughed suddenly, snorting a bit. "You guys called his *office*?"

"Yeah, how come?"

Looking at Fisher and Alex as though *they* were the aliens, she sighed. "Even FBI Agents have cell phones, nimrods."

"His *what*?" Fisher and Alex said in perfect unison, looking back up.

Veronica sighed, pulling out her phone. She looked up a number in a few seconds.

"Agent Mason?" she said after a moment. "This is Veronica Greenwich. Fisher and Alex have been trying to reach you. . . . Yes, that's what I told them. . . . I know! For geniuses they can be so absentminded sometimes."

She chuckled. Fisher stared dumbly at Alex and got the same dumb stare right back.

"He's been a little busy putting down a mutant snake rebellion in Arizona," Veronica said, hanging up. "But now that he knows we need his help, he's on his way."

Alex made a call to the MORONS base, asking to be picked up and taken back to the compound. A beat of silence passed as they all gloomily waited, and considered what might happen next. Fisher felt the weight of the situation settle onto his shoulders like a soaked wool blanket.

"Well, that's some good news, at least," Amanda said with a sigh. "Until Mason gets here, let's get our findings back to the super-villain who's trying to save the world."

"Yeah," Alex said, rolling his eyes. "And grab him a sandwich so he doesn't destroy it by accident."

A black SUV pulled up to the curb, and they boarded it in silence. They drove off to the NASA compound. It took some convincing, but they were able to talk the driver into making a quick stop at Fisher's favorite sandwich shop on the way. The Reuben on a hero roll was roughly the size of a shoebox. Fisher hauled it back to the car along with a big bag of chips for everyone else. They'd need the fuel for the work ahead.

Once again, they entered through the silo into the silent elevator. This time there was no dance lock. A blue glow pulsed off the walls as they at last emerged into the maze of walkways and stairways cutting across the artificial cavern.

"Fisher," Veronica said, leaning over the railing to look down into the open space. "Look at this."

The light was coming from the ship. Seven or eight panels along the length of its hull had illuminated, and the rhythmic deep blue wash was eerily hypnotic.

This time, they skipped on the laundry chute and took the spiral escalator near the center of the cavern. On the cavern floor, Dr. X was working on the ship with two other scientists and a dozen techs, who scurried back and forth with a variety of brightly polished instruments.

"Welcome back," Dr. X said, turning to greet them with a shallow grin. "I heard all about the parade antics on the news. The story going around had something to do with rampaging puppets."

"The Gemini have given up on staying incognito," said Alex. "They don't seem to care who notices. We need to get them off this planet, stat."

"It looks like you're making progress here, at least," Fisher said.

"Indeed," Dr. X said, clasping his slender hands in front of his chest. Fisher waited for him to say more, but after a moment Dr. X cleared his throat and nodded to the plastic bag Fisher was holding. Fisher sighed and removed the paper-wrapped sub from the bag, handing it over.

U.S. DEPARTMENT OF JUSTICE
FEDERAL BUREAU OF INVESTIGATION

SYD MASON
SPE

1 MOF
MOUN
555-2

MY CELL # 555-3386

The evil scientist unwrapped one end of the sandwich, inhaled deeply, and took a small bite. He chewed thoughtfully as Alex crossed his arms and Amanda started tapping her foot loudly.

"Excellent," said Dr. X, swallowing. "This will do perfectly. Now then, to the ship. Main power systems are online. We still can't get inside, however, but I dare say it should be space worthy before too much longer. Did you manage to track down the missing component portion?"

Alex set down his bag, opened it up, and pulled out the metal scanning device. "The missing *component* is a shuttle—and all of the data should be in here."

Dr. X picked up the scanner, turned it over in both

hands, and checked a small readout on its side. "The scanner's memory is full," he said. "Assuming the shuttle wasn't shielded in ways we can't anticipate, we should be able to learn everything we need to know about the ship's operating system."

"What happens then?" asked Fisher. A nearby worker fired up a welding torch to seal a small crack in the ship's hull and Fisher winced in the sudden flare.

"*Then* we try to bring the ship fully online," said Dr. X. "The question is, what do we do with it next? This cave is thickly shielded with thousands of tons of rock and our own concrete and lead barriers, but if we bring the ship up to the surface, the Gemini will know. And they *can't* know until we're ready to throw them a going-away party."

The flashes from the welding torch threw rapid, momentary shadows across Dr. X's face, as if he were a long-tormented soul rising from the underworld. It was an entirely appropriate look for him.

"If we can make Earth seem like too much trouble," Fisher said, "hopefully they'll want to leave. Thwarting their efforts at the parade was a good start. I think we should put together a presentation on everything wrong with the planet. Pollution, poisonous animals, the threat of asteroids, all that stuff. Presenting their repaired ship to them as a gift could seal the deal."

"And if they don't want to leave, maybe we can use it as a bargaining chip," Veronica added.

Dr. X nodded. "Precisely," he said. But Fisher thought he seemed hesitant, as if he didn't want to let the beautiful ship out of his clutches so soon. "You to your work, and I to mine."

He performed a comically elaborate bow. Amanda glared in reply and turned on her heel. Fisher and the others followed her back to the escalator.

"Oh! One more thing," Dr. X called after them. "Next time, I require a strawberry milk shake with a little paper umbrella. I know, I know, little umbrellas aren't normally put in milk shakes," he added, when Veronica started to object, "but I find them *awfully* charming."

A MORONS car dropped them outside of Wompalog's temporary home. Parade floats were still being taken apart as the cleanup effort continued. Afternoon classes were about to begin, and students weary from the parade were trudging to the classroom trailers. Fisher took a moment to realign his thoughts. For now, the Gemini were under control. They'd made their play to wreck the parade, and Fisher and the others had stopped them. Maybe the Gemini would start to realize that humans wouldn't be so easily pushed around—or turned into breakfast.

A defender, Fisher knew, doesn't have to destroy or even

defeat an attacker. He just has to make the attacker's job so hard that the win no longer seems worth it.

Maybe, just maybe, there was hope for Earth yet.

His phone buzzed. It was a text from his mother. At last, his parents were on their way back. As far as Fisher was concerned, they couldn't possibly get back fast enough. Fisher felt an extra surge of hope.

The text said, *We're almost home. Don't look up.*

Fisher looked up.

What he saw in the sky blotted that hope out like a waterlogged mattress dropping on a candle. The King of Hollywood lot was in shadow. A shadow cast by a massive spaceship floating directly overhead. The ground was vibrating.

The ship was rectangular, easily four times the size of the Gemini ship and bristling with dozens of extrusions, a good portion of which were probably weapons. The hull was painted a deep black, with an occasional lightning-bolt-like slash of bright red over it. Crudely scrawled writing appeared in several spots, and the glaring white skull of some very inhuman species was stenciled on the side, a pair of crossed blades beneath it.

A massive holographic image was projected from the belly of the ship and floated in the sky above the school. The hologram looked like a lobster that had been made from discarded engine parts. Everyone at school was staring dumbly up at the craft sitting in midair. It looked like it could turn Palo Alto into a mound of glowing pebbles with a single button push.

The other kids looked like they were trying to back away but had forgotten how to walk. Principal Teed stared up with a slack jaw, dropping the clipboard from his hand. Two news crews who'd been covering the parade rushed to put their equipment back together and grab a shot.

The lobster-hologram moved its mouth and made a series of clanky, static-like sounds. A translation boomed out a moment later. "Humans, your guests have something that belongs to us. If you value your lives and your planet, we will have it back. Now."

≋ CHAPTER 16 ≋

Space pirates. They're like ocean pirates, with a crucial difference—treading water doesn't help when you walk the plank.

—Vic Daring, Issue #89

"What . . . is . . . that?" Amanda let out. She backed up one step, as if to get out of the giant spacecraft's range.

Fisher knew, with a sinking feeling, that the Gemini were to these new aliens as tiger fish were to a tiger.

The real interplanterary heavy hitters had arrived. Fisher studied the incredible, massive machine above their heads. This ship wasn't designed to be pretty. Odds were, most of its targets never got the chance to see it.

Fisher had noticed before that the Gemini's compulsive planet-hopping covered more distance than it needed to. They skipped resource-rich planets to cover greater distance as they traveled. This was why. They weren't just consuming resources. They were *running* from their enemies, hiding out on various planets.

"Fisher." Alex pointed to a trio of dots that had appeared on the horizon. Fisher fished a long-range scope not much bigger than a jeweler's eyepiece from his pack, wondering if these new aliens had brought even *more* friends.

The scope focused automatically, and clean images came into view: narrow conical noses, clear canopies, long wings, and single tail fins.

"F-16s," Fisher said grimly. "There's no way air force radar could've missed this thing coming down through the atmosphere, and they've sent a welcoming party."

The fighter jets closed to about a thousand feet away and settled into a loop, making a broad circle around the ship like a cluster of asteroids caught in a planet's gravity. Fisher wondered if the pilots had made radio contact with whoever was inside.

After a few minutes, the underside of the huge craft lit up, and a broad green beam shone down to the middle of the lot, not far from where Fisher and the others stood. Fisher braced for the impact of a blast.

But the beam wasn't a weapon. Three figures descended as gently as if someone had turned down the Earth's gravity to near-zero levels . . . which, Fisher realized, was exactly what the beam was doing. The three beings touched down on the asphalt.

From the outside, at least, they looked completely mechanical. They had long, segmented bodies, insect-like faces with eyes on stalks, and a multitude of legs and arms. They looked, in fact, kind of like giant metal lobsters. Their many legs clacked and shifted on the ground, adjusting to their own weight as the beam turned off, and their long eyes—could they be cameras?—swiveled so that they appeared to be staring directly at Fisher. A hint of machine oil and coins met his nostrils.

A lead ball formed at the pit of Fisher's gut. Partially thanks to him, there was already one alien species well on its way to taking over Earth. Now, less than a week later, a second aggressive alien species had arrived. Still, he couldn't figure out why they were *here,* of all places. A temporary middle school location camped in trailers around a fast-food restaurant was one of the last places he'd expect.

Alex nudged Fisher.

"I think Earth may need our diplomacy again," he said quietly.

"Sure, because we know how well that's worked out so far," Fisher whispered. He wasn't just in over his head—he was standing at the bottom of a swimming pool dug into the bottom of the ocean, in pitch-black, being crushed to nothing by the pressure.

They were barely scraping together a plan to deal with the Gemini. What could they possibly do about the new-comers?

One of the creatures began to speak in its own incomprehensible language again. It sounded like someone clanking pots and pans at the other end of a really static-y phone connection. A speaker underneath its head played a translation that overlapped its sentence.

"Are you the representatives of Earth?"

Fisher and Alex exchanged a glance. In the distance, sirens were wailing. Fisher had no doubt that soon a squadron of cops, scientists, guards, and paratroopers would descend on the parking lot. Things could only go downhill. So Fisher nodded.

"Yes," Alex said confidently. "We simply want to establish peaceful relations."

"We have no issue with humans," said the alien, its transmitter crackling.

Fisher hoped he could believe them. "So what are you doing here?"

There was a short pause. "We are an independent crew of opportunistic spaceship raiders," said one of the alien lobsters.

"You're pirates," Veronica blurted.

The lobster tilted one black lens-tipped eyestalk to regard Veronica. A whirring sound followed by a click emitted from somewhere in its segmented body.

"Pirates," it said. "This word has been added to our database of your language."

"Great. So you want to loot our planet? Search for buried treasure?" asked Amanda.

"No. We are here only to seek justice from the other

AIRCRAFT
COMPARISON CHART

Mechastacean - scout ship

Gemini - stolen spacecraft

Humans - F-16

we're
DOOMED

beings on your planet, the—" The lobster pirate produced a wash of sound that Fisher just barely recognized as the Gemini's proper name. "Our scans indicated this spot as the rough epicenter of their activity."

So that was why they'd come here. Wompalog's temporary home was about halfway between Fisher's house and Loopity Land, and the Gemini had spent a lot of time here. The pirates weren't wasting any time in the pursuit of their prey.

"We call them the Gemini," said Fisher. "They crash-landed here a few days ago."

"The . . . Gemini," said the pirate, pausing as it assimilated the new word, "are in possession of something extremely valuable to us. Something that they stole en route to Earth. If you would direct us to their exact location . . . "

"Right here!" someone shouted. Fisher jumped and spun around. The Gemini, all twenty-six of them, were back. Their shuttle, now stripped of its parade decorations, hovered menacingly above the parking lot, and they were fanned out on the ground in front of it.

Confused voices rose up from the crowd, which had previously been struck completely dumb. Where did the Eastern European exchange students get a fancy-looking hovercraft? How did they know the robot aliens? *What in the world was happening?*

In the sky, the fighter jets were circling lower, probably debating what to do with their commanding officer. They couldn't fire at the aliens without putting all the people on the ground at risk. Even if they could damage the ship, what would happen if the massive structure exploded in the lower atmosphere over a populated area? It might be enough to wipe out the whole city.

"Um, you guys?" Veronica was looking back and forth between the Gemini and the space lobsters. "I'm thinking that standing between these two is *not* where we want to be right now."

"Agreed," Alex said. "Run!"

Alex grabbed Amanda's hand as they dashed behind the library trailer with Veronica and Fisher in tow. Everyone else—including the security guards—scrambled for cover. One of the pirates made a large step to the side. Fisher spotted one of its manipulator limbs slashing through the air in Veronica's direction. He had exactly enough time to shove her forward and out of the way, but he stumbled backward, right into the middle of the fight. Veronica turned back for him, but he shook his head at her terrified eyes.

Four of the Gemini charged across the lot at full sprint. The pirates fanned out, and sprouted extra limbs from inside their alloy shells. The limbs were tipped with blades and weapons Fisher couldn't even identify.

The Gemini leapt high into the air, far higher than a human could. As they hurtled toward the pirates, each pair of Gemini drones locked hands and transformed in mid-dive. By the time they hit their targets, four young girls had become two very tall and broad, if still cheerleader-like, girls. They landed heavily on one of the metal-lobster-alien-pirates, breaking into vicious brawls.

The third pirate backed off from its grappling comrades, inclining its head downward. A massive apparatus sprung from its back. Electricity raced across its surface as the weapon charged up.

The now-giant Gemini girls rolled along the ground, trying to tear into the pirates' armored sides with their massive, perfectly manicured and deadly nails. The pirates fought back with their many appendages, clutching and stabbing at the Gemini with piston-like limbs and grasping claws.

Every time Fisher took a step in one direction, one of the fighters would step or tumble in his way. He twisted in a dizzying circle, looking for an escape route.

Boom.

Fisher once again collapsed to his knees as the middle pirate fired off the enormous weapon affixed to its back. It felt like the noonday sun in August had just popped up, and the hairs on the back of his neck raised, full of static. The Gemini scattered out of the way just in time.

The beam struck the Gemini shuttle dead center. A lengthwise two-foot hole was cored out of it instantly, and the disabled craft crashed to the ground, its lights blinking insanely before going dark with a final whimper.

In the momentary pause that followed the explosion, Fisher ran, reaching the relative safety of the library trailer just as the Gemini, roaring with rage, resumed their attack. Veronica held Fisher tightly when he reached her.

"You all right?" she said hoarsely.

"Amazingly, yes," Fisher gasped. "The question is, will any of us be when this fight is over?"

Eight of the Gemini ran together and began morphing into a different shape: a solid white ball the size of a small car. The other eighteen Gemini clambered into a pile, similar to a cheerleader's pyramid, and within seconds had turned into a single giant figure, one with distinct arms, legs, and a head but no other features, like an unfinished statue. It looked like some kind of organic stone, almost polished.

The transformation left enough of a lull in the cacophony of battle that the screams and panicked shouts of the crowd became briefly audible again. The crowd clearly wanted to run, but they were too cowed by the spectacle to budge. They could only hunker down behind the trailers in terror.

The giant picked up the ball with one immense hand, wound up, and threw the glowing projectile at the pirates' ship. As it spun through the air, it emitted a familiar sound. This time it wasn't so much like popcorn popping as a line of firecrackers being set off.

Up and up and up it went, directly toward the pirate's ship.

Before it could make impact, four glittering particle beams stabbed down from the underside of the ship. One blast of energy hit the ball dead-on.

The light from the explosion forced Fisher's eyes shut, and the shock wave, hitting him a second later, made him stagger to his knees. The ship rocked slightly, and a small area on its underside gave off sparks. Even though the ball hadn't struck the ship directly, the nearby explosion had been enough to do significant damage.

The pirates retreated to the center of the parking lot.

"Do not think this is over," the pirate leader said. "There is nowhere you can go where we cannot find you. You *will* return what is ours." The green beam zipped the three lobsters back up far more quickly than it had set them down, and the ship flew away with a sonic boom.

With thundering engines, the F-16s chased after the pirate ship, heading for the horizon.

Fisher realized he'd been holding his breath and exhaled. The fight was over, and no one had been harmed—for now. But he knew they'd been lucky. The Gemini shuttle had been destroyed—and that was just a little skirmish. A full-scale battle could be devastating. An all-out war would decimate the planet.

The giant shape shifted back into eighteen girls. The secret was out now. Soon every news agency worldwide would be blaring this story. He wondered if some country would decide not to wait around and launch its own attack on one or both alien species. The possible bad endings to the situation had multiplied hugely.

Dozens of police cars both marked and unmarked pulled into the parking lot, sirens wailing. From one of them, Mr. and Mrs. Bas appeared. They dashed toward their kids.

"Is everyone all right?" Mr. Bas said.

Fisher nodded shakily. "Did you see the explosion?"

"From nearly a mile away," Mr. Bas said grimly. "If the explosion had occurred on the ground, everything within five blocks of here would be flattened."

"This is what the secret meeting was about," Mrs. Bas said, looking up at the sky as if waiting for every other species in the galaxy with a grudge to show up.

"We knew something else had arrived in the solar system," Mr. Bas said. "But we weren't sure it was another ship until we got to the Pentagon. We've been discussing possible options for dealing with these new aliens.

Frankly," he scratched the back of his neck, "we didn't come up with a whole lot."

"But what we do know, we're going to go tell the police," Mrs. Bas said. She smiled tensely at Fisher and Alex. "We'll see you boys as soon as we're done."

There was still a little haze cloud in the sky where the explosion had been. After a moment, Fisher realized there were little burning pieces of the ship's hull floating down to the ground.

"If they'd used more drones," Alex said, "the force of the blast could have been enormous. As in, *wiping out Palo Alto* enormous."

"So far, they've been exploding often enough to keep their numbers the same," Fisher said. "But if they go through a calm period for a while and start eating faster, they'll generate more and more drones. They could have that kind of power before too long."

Fisher saw the image in his head. The school flat, everyone he knew buried in rubble. They'd nearly brought the Gemini under control, only to meet these pirates. A situation that had been on the verge of improving now looked like it was going to get far worse. Fisher could still feel that huge ship looming over his head. Where would it appear next? And what could any of them do?

"I was afraid the Gemini were about to start a war

with *us*," said Fisher. "I didn't think they were already in one. With space pirates."

"But what do the space pirates want from the Gemini?" asked Amanda.

"The Gemini have something that belongs to them," said Alex. "Clearly, something very important. And obviously the Gemini aren't exactly itching to give it back."

Veronica blew out a long breath. "The question is, do we pick a side, or do we risk turning *both* sets of angry aliens against us?"

CHAPTER 17

There is no more decisive a statement of superiority over another species than to consider them your breakfast.
—Three, Cell Wall Writings

In all of human history there had been not a single recorded instance of contact with an extraterrestrial species—and now Palo Alto had met *two* alien species in a matter of days. In the blink of an eye, the Gemini problem had blown up into the problem of a major potential interstellar war. And now everyone knew what the Gemini were, and what they were really capable of. Without even using any technology, they had damaged a skyscraper-sized space battleship. An explosion hundreds of feet away had almost knocked everyone at Wompalog flat on their backs.

As various traumatized kids and teachers were shepherded into ambulances for routine checkups—or merely made a beeline for their waiting cars—Fisher approached Anna and Bee, who were standing with the other Gemini in the parking lot, examining their nails as though nothing had happened. The closer he got to them, the harder his heart raced—still, he forced himself to get going, planting himself squarely in front of Anna.

"The pirates spoke of an item you stole from them," he said, trying to keep the tremor from his voice. "Do you know what they meant?"

"They are pirates," Anna replied, shrugging. "In their view, whatever they want belongs to them. Clearly, they have decided they want something of ours. We don't know what."

"Fisher!" Mrs. Bas jogged across the parking lot, drawing Fisher back from Anna as if worried the drone would spontaneously combust in his face. Which wasn't exactly an unfounded worry. "It's, er, time to go home. For *all* of us." She gestured pointedly to the Gemini's specially outfitted bus, which had just rumbled up to the parking lot. Fortunately, the Gemini didn't resist. They turned and, without another word, filed onto the bus.

Fisher, Alex, Veronica, and Amanda rode back in near silence to the Bas house with Fisher's parents, tailing the gleaming bus as it dodged through side streets. Traffic near the school had ground to a halt as news crews and police vehicles continued to swarm the spot.

Fisher crossed his arms tightly. He knew that if he put his hands somewhere, they'd start twitching and rattling like he was playing an invisible floating piano.

"Do you think it could be the spaceship that they

want?" Veronica spoke up suddenly. "We know the Gemini stole it from someone."

Mrs. Bas sighed and shook her head. "We don't think so," she said. "The spaceship's interior doesn't look as though it could accommodate the pirates' bodies. Whatever they're after, it isn't that." She cleared her throat and exchanged a glance with Mr. Bas. "The *good* news is we have the best and the brightest minds working on the problem."

If the *best* included Dr. X, Fisher thought darkly, they were in deep trouble.

But only a few minutes later, when Fisher walked through his front door, he saw what his mother meant. Standing in the living room, clearly waiting for them, was a tall man in a dark suit.

"Agent Mason!" Alex cried as they walked into the room. Fisher's hopes of dealing with the extraterrestrial threats that kept appearing out of nowhere lifted considerably.

"Hello, ladies, gentlemen," Mason said, smiling. "Seems like you've had a busy week."

"Finally," asked Alex, detaching Paul from his ankles and dropping onto the couch. Amanda joined him, leaning into his shoulder. Fisher gave the cheerful FP a scratch behind his ears, careful not to disturb the still tender one. "We could have used *assistance* before the Gemini tried to turn the Thanksgiving parade into a fireworks show."

"I've been pretty busy myself," Mason said. "You should see what a few decades of nuclear testing can do to a diamondback population. But that's taken care of now. Like my new kicks?" He pointed down at the brand-new pair of snakeskin boots he was wearing. They didn't exactly match the suit, but they certainly made a statement. And that statement was, *If you are making a list of people to mess with, you might want to leave this man's name off it.*

"And while I was busy in the desert, my colleagues have been busy tracking the new ship," said Agent Mason. "Astronomers detected it coming into the solar system a few days ago. We think the pirates were tracking the Gemini. The M3 beacon helped the Gemini to find us . . . and the pirates to find *them*. The pirates are keeping very close tabs on the Gemini. They haven't even left the West Coast."

"Where's the pirate ship now?" Fisher asked. He felt a fresh shot of adrenaline slip into his bloodstream.

"Hovering over the Pacific, close enough to San Francisco to be visible to the naked eye from Fisherman's Wharf," Agent Mason said, his expression grim. "We've got jets patrolling the Bay twenty-four-seven, but there's no way of knowing how much damage they could do even if we deployed them. The ship hasn't answered any attempts at contact. What we need to do is get someone on that ship. Unfortunately, since it's floating in midair, it's impossible to sneak up to undetected. We'd have to trick them into letting someone aboard."

Fisher considered the problem for a moment. If the pirates weren't responding to radio contact, there wasn't much reason to think that they'd want to talk to a human. Of course, it wasn't the *humans* they were here for in the first place . . .

Agent Mason was staring at Fisher, like an expectant teacher waiting for a particular result. It was obvious that he already had a solution to propose.

"The pirates want to deal with the Gemini," Alex said slowly, puzzling it out. He looked up, smiling. "So why don't we give them Gemini? And in their preferred human form . . . *twins*." He put a hand on Fisher's shoulder.

"You're not seriously . . . " Veronica began, wide-eyed.

"He is seriously," Amanda said, sighing. "Trust me. And, much as I hate to say it, I can't really think of a better idea."

Fisher opened his mouth but all that emerged was a squeak. Going in disguise as one alien species to negotiate with another alien species? It was crazy. It was completely crazy. That said . . . it might just be the best idea they had.

In fact, it might be the *only* idea they had.

"That is exactly what I had in mind," Mason said with a proud smile.

"What??" said both Bas parents in unison.

MECHASTACEAN
SCOUT SHIP LOCATION

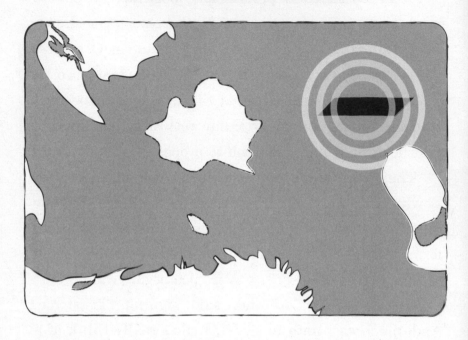

"Just think for a moment," Mason said, holding up a hand. "Fisher and Alex have experience working together inside enemy-controlled facilities. They have more experience at it than most FBI agents, in fact. They've proven themselves capable of great ingenuity in high-stress situations. And they've had more face-to-face contact with the Gemini than anybody. They know how they act and speak."

Fisher's mom and dad looked at one another worriedly. Veronica looked at Fisher, clearly hoping to hear a better idea come out of his mouth. Fisher wished he had one for her. Amanda's face was set with solemn determination.

"You may be right," Mrs. Bas said hesitantly. "If you really think it's the best way, and if you two are really up for it . . . maybe. Just let us think a little."

Mason nodded.

"Of course." The spy turned back to Fisher and Alex. "But in the meantime . . . you boys wouldn't happen to know your wig size, would you?"

≋ CHAPTER 18 ≋

DIPLOMACY: THE ART OF SAYING WORDS YOU
DON'T MEAN TO PEOPLE YOU DON'T LIKE, TO
GET THINGS YOU DON'T DESERVE.
— SYD MASON, FBI MEMO

"Are you sure we have to do this?" Fisher said, scratching his head through the luxurious blond tresses of the wig that Agent Mason's FBI disguise artist had clipped to his real hair. The young man was busily applying eyeliner and rouge to Alex's face. "The Gemini can look like anything. Why can't we just go as ourselves?"

After a lifetime of being teased, harassed, and generally tormented, Fisher really wasn't enjoying the wig-and-lipstick look. He dreaded even the *tiny* possibility that one of the Vikings would see him like this. And truth be told—he did not make a very pretty girl.

But he knew this was the most important mission he'd ever been on—maybe the most important mission in all of human history. His concerns were tiny by comparison.

Still, he made a plan to vaporize any cameras he noticed on site until he was out of disguise.

"For one thing," Mason said, "the pirates have

already seen you. And even though they're probably terrible at telling humans apart, it's safer to change your appearance. For another thing, the Gemini have been mostly assuming girl form during their time on Earth. It's what the pirates expect to see. They're less likely to ask questions."

Amanda's and Veronica's parents had both come to collect them. Fisher feared, given their responses to the news coverage of the aliens' fight, neither family would ever let their daughters out of the house again. The boys were sitting on a pair of stools in the living room, with the suitcase-sized disguise kit wide open on the floor in front of them.

FP looked up at the brothers and cocked his head, his ears twitching a little with curiosity. A pair of tentacles appeared from around the corner of the couch, and Paul glided around FP, gazing up with his deep black eyes. FP turned around and bumped Paul's bulbous head with his snout, and the octopus responded with a little ripple of his ten limbs.

Fisher fiddled with the embroidered hem of his light blue skirt, which fell just below his knees. His white turtleneck made him feel like he was being throttled by a rag doll. At least he was wearing flats. Nothing would mess up interspecies negotiations like tripping in wedge heels before they'd gotten through the airlock.

Fisher pulled on a strand of his wig and the gentle curl sprang back up. He pulled it again, and watched the coil oscillate up and down. $F = -kx$, the harmonic oscillation equation. Physics always calmed him down.

"How do I look?" said Alex. Fisher brushed his new hair out of his eyes. He looked over at his clone, amazed.

"You look like a girl," Fisher said, marveling.

"You're pretty convincing yourself," Alex said. He was wearing the exact same wig and outfit as Fisher. The disguise artist had even given Alex a third freckle on his nose to match Fisher exactly.

"I smell like an entire florist shop was just hurled at me," said Fisher.

"I smell like a bakery," said Alex. "I'm kinda liking it. Maybe I should invest in some pastry-scented colognes."

Fisher pursed his lips, trying to catch a glimpse of the soft pink coating that now encased them: Petunia 37, according to the lipstick tube.

"Is this stuff volatile at all?" he said. "Reactive? Are there any substances I should avoid?"

"Just dignity, I think," Alex said.

"You're both very fetching," Mason said with a smile. Fisher brushed a crease out of his skirt. "Ready?"

Alex nodded, followed by Fisher. Each of them shouldered a small handbag concealing a few gadgets and potentially useful items.

Mr. and Mrs. Bas, who had been consulting with several colleagues in the kitchen, entered the room and stopped short, their mouths unhinging.

"You—you look so beautiful," their mom said, and she sniffed, wiping a real tear away from her eye.

Mr. Bas put an arm around her shoulder. "Are you certain this is the only way?" he said.

"It's the only way short of launching an attack," said Mason. "Your boys are going to keep a lot of people from getting hurt."

"Is there any way we can help?" Mrs. Bas said.

"We'll be okay," Fisher promised—a promise he hoped he wouldn't have to break. Sneaking onto an enemy spaceship, dressed as a teenage girl, wasn't exactly an ideal plan.

The Bas parents were themselves disguised in perfectly tailored navy officer uniforms. They had insisted on going with Agent Mason to take their sons to the ship, and he'd insisted on this condition.

"Okay," Fisher said, flipping his hair over his shoulder. "Let's go negotiate."

A car was waiting for them right outside the house, and sped them to the coast. Too soon, it pulled up beside an almost invisible footpath, which led straight through a cliff to a tiny dock covered by blue and gray camouflage netting. A small boat in the same color scheme was waiting for them.

Agent Mason, Fisher, Alex, and their parents boarded the boat. A crew of three was already aboard. Fisher staggered a little bit as the craft launched, trying to adjust for the rolling of the deck. The sky was gray above the smooth sea, and the cold mist of spray dampened his face and his fake blond hair.

"We packed this for you," said Mr. Bas, indicating a large duffel bag he'd brought. "It has a transmitter as powerful as a major radio station. If you get in trouble just hit the big button and we'll know. There are also two parachutes inside. Slip them on, jump, and they'll deploy automatically as soon as you need them."

Fisher forced a smile. They knew he'd been through tougher spots than this and gotten out okay, but this was the first time they were actually knowingly sending him into danger. If he didn't come back, they would blame themselves as long as they lived.

But he would be okay. It was a simple job. Just pretend to be an alien species' hive drone and conduct negotiations with a totally different alien species over a dispute he knew nothing about.

Yep, simple.

The boat started to kick a little more as the waves got higher farther from shore. It was almost evening. In the distance to the right was the opening of the San Francisco Bay, and directly ahead of them was a dark smudge in the sky, a stark shadow against the setting sun.

"There it is," Mason said. He pulled out a pair of binoculars and gazed at the ship. "Totally motionless. Imagine the kind of power it must take to keep an object that size hovering in midair for days on end."

Ordinarily Fisher would've been able to estimate the ship's mass and calculate the amount of power it would take to the tenth of a joule. But the closer they got to the huge vessel, the more unsteady his brain felt. It seemed that no matter how many crazily dangerous situations he encountered, he was still scared.

To their right, the bay came into view, and they could see San Francisco and Oakland winding down their busy days as evening rush hour set in. Fisher thought about how many people lived there. Millions in the SF area alone. Millions more in LA, Sacramento, San Diego, back home in Palo Alto. Then farther away, Seattle, Austin, Chicago, New York, Boston, Atlanta . . . all of those people. Every single one of them was threatened by the Gemini and by these pirates. As fear and doubt crept their spiky tentacles into Fisher's thoughts, he kept naming cities, practically chanting in his head, as the ship got bigger and bigger ahead and above them. London, Berlin, São Paolo, Hong Kong, Calcutta, Nairobi . . .

He could help all of them. He had to help all of them.

Mason pulled a small hand radio out of an inside pocket.

"Attention, vessel. My name is Syd Mason, and I am a representative of the local human government. We have gotten the Gemini to agree to in-person negotiations. We are bringing them to you now, in the interest of peace for all. Please respond."

Five seconds passed. Ten, thirty, then a minute, then five. A shadow fell over the boat. Fisher gazed up at the black-and-red monster of a ship. It looked like a windowless black tower turned on its side—and covered in guns. He wondered if the pirates would refuse, if he and everyone on the boat were about to be turned into a mist as fine as the sea spray around them.

Syd's radio crackled, sending a shock up Fisher's backbone.

"Confirmed," a deep, synthesized voice responded. "Hold your position and stand away from the Gemini representatives."

"Good luck," Mrs. Bas whispered. She inched closer to them, obviously seized by a powerful urge to hug the boys. But she quickly backed away, careful to maintain their cover.

"You'll do great," said Mr. Bas, his voice catching a little in his throat, patting each of them on the shoulder once.

"Clear a space," Mason said. He, Fisher's parents, and the crew backed away as far as the little boat allowed, and Fisher and Alex stepped forward. Fisher kept a tight grip on the duffel bag.

There was a very slight warmth on Fisher's face, and the sea scents in the air disappeared. Even the sounds around them dulled. A smooth, almost comforting hum greeted their ears. Suddenly, everything was green. Fisher and Alex were standing in the center of a column of light.

The antigravitational beam.

A moment later Fisher and Alex became weightless. They floated upward gently. The tension in Fisher's muscles vanished as the Earth released its pull on them. Other than the lack of water, it felt a lot like being in a swimming pool. Alex smiled and swung his arms from side to side, turning himself.

"Can we get one for our house?" he said, turning a somersault in the weightless beam. Fisher looked out over the ocean as they continued floating higher. He saw the waves getting bigger and more turbulent as the ocean went farther out, whitecaps dotting the deep blue. He even saw the spray of a pod of whales. Everything was dyed the emerald tone of the beam, making Fisher feel like he was watching it on an insanely high-definition screen with a custom color filter turned on.

The view was cut off by complete darkness as the battleship swallowed them. Moments later, they popped up into some kind of receiving deck. A hatch snapped shut beneath them and the beam's emitter, a complex arrangement of circuits and lenses in the ceiling, went dark.

Fisher and Alex settled to the floor. The hexagonal room was mostly bare, a utilitarian construction of black and gray metal. There were shelves and equipment racks on all six walls, although they were currently empty.

They were in the belly of the beast now. Agent Mason and the others couldn't pull them from the mission even if they wanted to. The fact that there was no longer any option of turning back helped ease Fisher's fear. His course was set, and he would follow it—whatever the result.

He couldn't tell where the dim light was coming from. There was a deep, rhythmic hum in the air, undoubtedly the ship's engines. The air tasted like dusty pennies. Fisher wondered whether the pirates, who at least *looked* like robots, needed to breathe, or whether the atmosphere inside the ship had been calibrated just for them. Of course, even if the pirates were mechanical, it was possible they needed a pressurized environment to work properly.

A doorway appeared in one wall as a hatch opened silently. Fisher started to say something but bit down on his tongue to stop himself. The Gemini had one brain. Two Gemini drones talking to one another would be like Fisher talking to his hand to get it to pick something up.

It would give them away immediately.

Alex took the lead, rolling his shoulders forward in a show of bravado that was funny, given his blond wig and skirt. Fisher tried to mirror Alex's posture exactly.

The hatch led to a long, dark corridor with a trapezoidal shape, the walls sloping inward as they went up, resulting in a ceiling narrower than the floor. As far as Fisher could see, the walls and floor were totally featureless. The ceiling, however, was studded with what looked like plugs and input terminals.

Two of the lobsters were waiting for them at a corridor intersection. Up close, Fisher could see that they both had greenish hues to their metal-and-plastic exoskeletons, and their stalk eyes swiveled and clicked, looking over Fisher and his clone.

"This is the first time," one of them said in a droning voice, "that we have made in-person contact with you. We do not speak your language, nor you ours. It is fortunate we have both learned this human tongue." Inwardly, Fisher let out a sigh as strong as a gale. He hadn't even thought about the language issue. "However, as this is our first meeting with two of your drones, we will require proof that you are, indeed, Gemini."

Fisher's relief immediately turned to terror. What could they do to prove they were something they weren't?

"We are, of course, aware of your ability to physically

MECHASTACEAN FIGURE

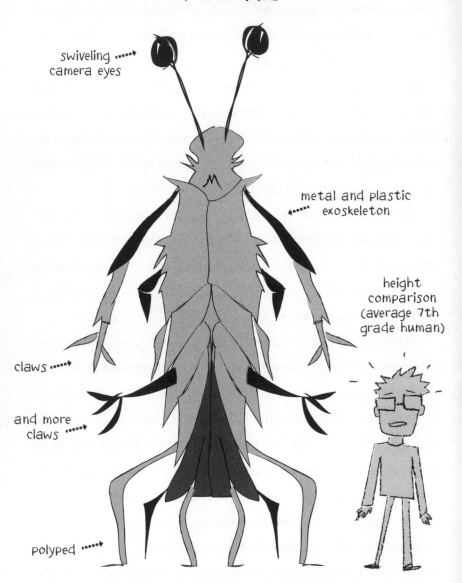

swiveling camera eyes

metal and plastic exoskeleton

height comparison (average 7th grade human)

claws

and more claws

polyped

transform." Fisher imagined he saw the lobster frown, and wondered whether it was recalling the massive ball of fiery light that had nearly taken out the mother ship. "Demonstrate this ability, and we will continue our discussion."

Fisher's mind raced through a long list of possible excuses he could give them. Too humid? They needed direct sunlight? They just weren't feeling very transform-y today? There had to be *something* in the duffel bag that could help them . . . .

Fisher turned to look at Alex. Alex, keeping up the act, mirrored his motion. Fisher winked extremely slightly, and spoke in the most toneless, most Gemini-like voice he could summon.

"Of course," he said flatly. "We shall be happy to demonstrate. This planet's gravity does make the transformation more difficult, of course. We must execute an exact sequence of motion."

He gave Alex the tiny wink again, and slowly raised his left arm. Alex mirrored perfectly. He put his right arm behind Alex's back, Alex again copying him flawlessly, and they walked in a slow circle.

As they moved, Fisher's hidden right hand slipped into Alex's handbag, felt around for a moment, and pulled out one of Alex's infamous trick tissues. They'd become infamous during an incident in Principal Teed's office. He brushed it softly against Alex's arm to let him know what was about to happen.

Fisher stopped and raised his right arm high, tissue concealed in his fist. Alex's followed suit. At a wink from Fisher, they plunged their right arms downward, and Fisher released the tissue, filling the corridor with smoke. He yanked Alex and the duffel bag into the corridor on the left side of the intersection.

The tightness of the space made the smoke linger. As it did, Fisher and Alex were pulling off their wigs, turtlenecks, and skirts as fast as they could. They hastily wiped their makeup off with the cleaning wipes in the bag, stuffed their disguise inside, then slipped on the change of jeans and T-shirts within.

"Nice work," Alex whispered in Fisher's ear. They snuck back into the intersection just as the smoke began to clear. A few seconds later, full visibility returned. Fisher calmly glanced at Alex and realized there was a small lipstick smudge just below his mouth. He held his breath, waiting for the death rays to start blasting. But the pirate robo-lobsters—or whatever they were—actually looked impressed.

"Very clever," the same one said. "You take the form of the human diplomats who helped arrange this meeting. That is sufficient. You may remain in this form and we can discuss our conflict."

"Indeed," Fisher said in his drone voice, "let us speak." He searched for a way to find out what it was the Gemini had taken without revealing that he didn't know. "We . . . are uncertain of the significance of the item that you want returned. What can it truly matter to you?"

"The chip you stole is one of a kind. We lost the ability to replicate them centuries ago," the pirate replied, a few spindly things around its mouth clicking together. "When your ship intercepted one of our transports, you may have thought the chip only a sample of our technology, a useful item we could easily replace. It is the key to the Mother Machine, the centerpiece of Mechastacean civilization."

Mechastacean. Fisher filed away the word in his mind. So the closest English translation of their name did in fact mean "robot lobster."

"The Mother Machine is what regulates and debugs our programming, as well as overseeing repairs and maintenance," the Mechastacean leader said. "If she were to shut down, we would eventually succumb to errors and physical breakdown. It would spell the end of our kind."

Fisher found it tough to conceal his emotional reaction to the news. The Gemini had stolen a vital part of the Mechastacean civilization, dooming an entire species in the process. Could they have *eaten* the chip? It was possible. But since the Gemini could eat almost anything, he couldn't see them going to the trouble to steal something as valuable as the chip just to devour it. He only knew now, more than ever, that the Gemini had to be stopped. Not just for Earth, but for the whole galaxy.

"Well," Alex said. "Perhaps we can come to an agreeable arrangement."

"We already have an arrangement," the leader said. "And I strongly suggest you agree to it. You have one Earth day, starting the moment you leave this ship, to return the chip to us. The control chip is everything to us. Be warned that we have brought far more than this scout frigate, and will do anything to ensure its return."

Fisher hoped his eyes hadn't visibly boggled. This vast, ground-shaking behemoth was a *scout ship*? What would a cruiser look like? Or a battleship?

"There is a full Mechastacean fleet waiting just outside this solar system. It can be here within hours, and it possesses more than enough firepower to burn the surface of this world to cinders, incinerating all of the organic materials you have come here to feed upon."

"Maybe . . . " Alex began, his voice quivering slightly, "if we were to—"

"One day," the Mechastacean interrupted him. "Go."

A hatch slammed shut between Fisher and Alex and the pirates. Fisher again suppressed the urge to talk to

Alex. They had to maintain their Gemini cover until they were safely away from the ship.

Still, Fisher and Alex exchanged a glance that communicated everything they needed to say. As spies, they'd been a complete success. The Mechastaceans hadn't seen through their disguise and they'd learned a great deal of information.

Unfortunately, the information was that they and everyone they knew, not to mention everyone they didn't know, had only twenty-four hours to live.

CHAPTER 19

Have a little perspective: I never tried to eat anyone's planet.

—Dr. X, upon release by Syd Mason

The boat tore across the choppy waves.

"A computer chip, huh?" Syd Mason said, stroking his chin, after Fisher and Alex had given him and their parents the short version of the story.

"Apparently, the chip contains the key to the Mechastacean civilization," Fisher said, blinking as the saltwater spray kicked up in his eyes. "I think the Gemini stole it to use as insurance, to keep the Mechastaceans from coming after them."

"And obviously, just the opposite happened," Alex said. "But it doesn't matter *why*. All that matters is getting the chip back from the Gemini and into the hands of its owners."

"But how?" Fisher said. "The chip could be anywhere."

"True," Mason said. "But at least we have some new firepower on our side. Dr. X has hacked into the Gemini ship's computer. It may well be able to tell us where the chip is hidden."

Twenty minutes later, Fisher and Alex were staring at the now-familiar shape of the Gemini ship. Next to the Mechastacean frigate, it looked as small as a child's toy. More lights had come on around its hull, and a thick cable had been attached to it with a large, ugly-looking adapter box.

"The chip's not in there," Dr. X said, his face lit up a creepy faint blue from the screen he was consulting.

"Are you sure?" said Alex.

"Positive," X replied. "The ship's records are incredibly detailed. Using this handy translator, I can review a log of every single thing that has ever come on board. The chip was logged into the ship's cargo hold some time ago, but it was removed shortly before the Gemini attempted to land on Earth."

"And you're certain the ship's computer isn't fooling you?" Mr. Bas said, crossing his arms. "The Gemini are trying to keep it hidden, after all. You can't always stop at the surface level."

"*Mister* Bas, my self-replicating AIs have sifted through every picometer of hard drive space on this ship," Dr. X said.

"Self-replicating AIs," Mrs. Bas half snorted. "Unreliable. They could be erasing the data you're looking for without proper oversight."

"You wouldn't know proper oversight if it brained you

with a stale cabbage and locked you in a trunk," Dr. X said just barely loud enough to be heard.

"Hey. *Hey!*" Mason said. "Future of the human species, people. Let's focus. The point is, the chip is not here."

Fisher felt the urge to kick something, but managed to restrain himself. Each piece of equipment down here was probably worth more than a King of Hollywood franchise.

But the clock was ticking. There *had* to be a way to get the chip.

Alex started to pace. Then he paused mid-stride, planted his feet, and stared up at the ship.

"Wait a minute," he said. "I keep thinking of the diagram you showed us of the Gemini's growth patterns. Once they got this ship, they started eating their way across the universe, digesting worlds down to nothing."

Fisher's heart jumped a little as he latched right on to his clone's train of thought.

"When there's no more food, they get back in their ship and move on . . . " Fisher said.

"But if they didn't have their ship," Alex said, eyes gleaming, "they'd be stuck. Stuck on a barren planet they themselves turned into a desert."

Dr. X's mouth hitched into a slow smile. "They would starve to death."

"Yes," Mr. Bas said. "I . . . " He swallowed hard. "Agree."

"Me too," said Mrs. Bas like she had a spear at her back. "And, contrary to what recent events might make you believe, spacefaring species are very rare. The odds of another ship that they could hijack coming along are extremely remote."

"That is . . . correct," admitted Dr. X. He and the Bas parents exchanged a look of what seemed like mutual respect. Extremely reluctant, forced respect, but respect nevertheless.

The drive to the Bas house was short, fast, and utterly oblivious to all traffic laws. Armored cars plowed ahead, clearing the road for them. Fisher jumped from the car as soon as it had come to a stop.

Since the parking lot incident, FBI tactical units had been stationed around the Gemini bus, armed and ready for any signs of disturbance.

"Stand down, stand down," Agent Mason said, waving an arm and gesturing Fisher and Alex through the crowd. The squad lowered their weapons by centimeters, but they weren't letting the Gemini out of their sights.

Fisher and Alex knocked on the door of the Gemini bus. Immediately, it *whooshed* open, revealing Anna and Bee.

"Hello," Anna said, "this is unexpected. I suppose you have come to—"

"Stop," Fisher said, holding up a hand. "Enough with the human act. We know who you are, we know how you work, and we know what you're trying to do."

"And we know you have the Mechastacean chip," said Alex.

"We don't know why you stole it and we don't care," resumed Fisher. "But we do know you're not safe from the Mechastaceans—not here, not *anywhere*, unless you return the chip. Otherwise they'll wipe you out." He took a deep breath. "We need the chip, and we need it now. We will return it to the Mechastaceans on your behalf. They'll leave you alone, and they'll leave us alone. Otherwise, we're all goners."

Anna and Bee settled into a familiar reddish glow. A faint crackling underscored the visual change. More Gemini appeared behind them, and they began to glow as well.

"We are not convinced," Bee said. Both drones had their arms flat to their sides, the features on their faces swirling like Velveeta cheese, no longer trying to look at all human.

"Maybe this will convince you," Alex said, undaunted. His next few words would be crucial not just if they wanted the chip, but if they didn't want to get vaporized right now. "We know how you operate. You fly your stolen ship to a new planet, you grow and grow as you consume whatever that planet holds. As the supplies dwindle, you shrink back down again, until the threat of starvation forces you to move on." The crackle was louder now, and Alex had to speak up just to be heard over it. "But guess what? *We have your ship now.* We can destroy it. Even if you take over Earth, when you eventually drain it dry, you'll have no way to escape. You'll be trapped on a barren wasteland."

He stopped talking. Only the crackle broke the silence, roiling on like a bonfire. Fisher clenched his fists and held them against his legs, forcing himself not to run. He could *not* back down.

The crackle got a little quieter. The red light got dimmer. The other drones backed away into the bus. Anna and Bee closed their eyes, and the pulsing light went out. Silence returned.

"Fine," Anna said at last. "We will hand over the chip . . . *if* you return our vessel."

"As soon as the Mechastaceans leave the solar system, it's yours," Fisher said, holding a hand out for Anna to shake.

Instead, she placed her right hand on her stomach, and *pushed*. As Fisher gaped, her hand slid into her torso like she'd placed it in Jell-O. When she removed it, it held a piece of metal about the size and shape of a paperback novel. She handed it to Fisher. It had a very thin coating of green goop on it, but Fisher was too shocked to care.

"I didn't imagine I'd be saying this," Fisher said, blowing out a long breath, "but you may have just saved the planet."

≋ CHAPTER 20 ≋

Progress emerges from chaos. Which is what I told my teachers after I blew the school up.

—Fisher Bas, Personal Notes

Wednesday morning, Agent Mason stood just outside of the NASA base, surrounded by other vehicles and dozens of FBI agents in full SWAT gear. Fisher and Alex's parents were there as well, wearing the same military uniforms as when they'd gone along to the pirate ship.

To Fisher's shock and pleasure, both Veronica and Amanda had been allowed to come too—*with* their parents, who looked less than thrilled to be standing on a government-owned military compound, awaiting the arrival of an alien species. Veronica hugged Fisher like he was an almost-empty toothpaste tube. Amanda greeted Alex much the same way.

The night before, Fisher had returned to the base with the chip, and Mason had contacted the Mechastaceans immediately. The robot lobster pirates had requested a handoff the following morning. Fisher couldn't figure out why they'd wanted to wait, but the only thing that mattered was that a handoff *would* happen before the deadline the Mechastaceans had given them.

"You ready?" Mason said.

"We're ready," Alex said, holding up the chip.

Mason took off his mirrored aviators and looked over the shining—if still a bit gloppy and green—piece of alien technology. He nodded after a moment and tapped his earpiece.

"Make the call," he said. He looked at Fisher. "My people are contacting the Mechastacean ship right now. Their representatives will be at a predesignated meeting point in a few short minutes." He gestured to a large SUV. "Hop in, all of you."

Mrs. Bas sat up front with Mason. Mr. Bas sat in the middle seats with Alex and Amanda. Veronica and Fisher took seats in the very back, and the Cantrells, along with Veronica's parents, followed in a second SUV.

"What you kids have done is absolutely amazing," Mr. Bas said, putting an arm around Alex's shoulders.

"Thanks, Dad," Alex said. "We're just doing our best to help."

"Your best is pretty impressive," Mrs. Bas said, turning to look at her sons. Fisher smiled back at her.

"Thanks for believing in us," he said.

"You've earned it," she replied.

"How much time is on the clock?" Alex asked.

"Just over four hours," Mason said, glancing into the

MECHASTACEAN
COMPUTER CHIP

25% actual size!

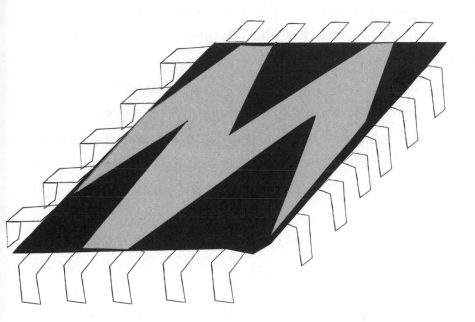

rearview mirror to look at Alex. "As long as this exchange goes smoothly, we'll be golden. If anything goes wrong, though . . . it'll be far too late."

"No pressure, then," Alex mumbled.

They pulled onto the road with two other FBI vehicles leading the way in front of them and two more bringing up the rear, behind the vehicle containing Amanda's parents and Veronica's mom.

Fisher heard a rumble in the air and pressed his

forehead to the window, expecting to see more other-worldly spacecraft. Instead he saw five jet fighters flying in a tight V formation above them. Others were appearing on the horizon. At the third intersection their convoy passed, a squad of soldiers was setting up sandbags on one corner of the sidewalk. Armored vehicles were rumbling into position on the larger streets.

Fifteen minutes passed, and they left the city behind. On a gently sloping hillside, a battery of surface-to-air missiles had been set into place on thick steel legs like a giant spider rearing up and presenting its fangs to the sky. The military was gathering to repel an invasion.

Fisher felt a steel cable tightening around his chest. He knew that if anything went wrong, there wouldn't *be* an invasion. The Mechastaceans would just sit in high orbit and bombard the planet until nothing was left but radioactive dust.

Veronica put her hand on his and gave him a reassuring smile.

"Don't worry," she said. "Everything's going to be fine—thanks to you."

"Yeah," Fisher said, looking down at his lap. He wondered whether the whole mess would have started if not for him. He'd welcomed the Gemini to the planet with open arms. He'd been the one to ride the M3 in the first place.

"You're thinking that this is your fault, aren't you?" Veronica said pointedly.

Fisher gaped at her. "How can you tell?"

"I know you, Fisher," Veronica said. Fisher continued to be kind of surprised by that fact. The idea that anyone his age would want to get to know him was still new. Especially when the person in question was Veronica.

"Well, maybe a little," Fisher said as the car turned down a dirt road. Apparently, the meeting was going to be in the middle of nowhere.

"It's true that you and Alex were excited by the chance to introduce earth to aliens—very pretty ones, too," she said. Fisher blushed and looked down. "But the Gemini have been studying us for years. They were going to land at *some* point. No matter where they landed or who they met. I for one think it's lucky that they landed near someone as smart and courageous as you . . . and me, of course," she said slyly.

Fisher smiled. She had a point. "Thank you," he said, half sighing, trying to breathe as much tension out of his body as he could. He needed to focus. He would meet with the Mechastaceans one last time, secure the deal, and then it would be done. The pirates would leave—and hopefully the Gemini would realize that unless they left, too, the humans would never return their ship.

"Look alive," Mason said. "We're almost there."

Two Mechastaceans were standing in the middle of a small field, next to a shuttlecraft of their own. The shuttle had broad, forward-swept wings and a jutting central cockpit. It rested on a trio of long landing struts.

"Okay," Mason said. "Boys, you know what to do."

"Let me know if you need a little more forceful persuasion," Amanda said to Alex, putting her right fist into her left palm.

"I will, don't worry," said Alex, squeezing her arm.

"Good luck, boys," said Mr. Bas.

"We'll be right behind you," Mrs. Bas said.

The vehicle came to a stop, and Agent Mason got out, immediately followed by Fisher's parents. Four of the other cars that had escorted them came to a halt and all of their doors popped open instantly, spilling heavily armed, armored FBI tactical teams out onto the field. The teams fanned out and created a wide semicircle facing the Mechastaceans. They kept their weapons pointed at the ground, but they were visibly tensed.

A pair of low-flying Apache helicopters crested a nearby hill, coming up quickly on their position and hovering over the FBI vehicles.

Alex clasped Amanda's hand and stepped out of the SUV. Veronica leaned over and gave Fisher a kiss on the cheek.

"Good luck," she said.

"Thanks," Fisher said, and followed Alex out of the car.

It was disturbing to Fisher that the robots did not fidget. Fisher had still not gotten used to this, though it made sense. If a robot didn't have something to do, it did not move. And the Mechastaceans, even if they were a species of sorts, with their own civilization, goals, and perhaps emotions, were robots. The two representatives stood waiting like a metal sculptor had built them on the spot years ago and then forgotten about them. Their three-clawed, grasping arms sparkled. Multiple sets of limbs kept them perfectly stable. At three points, one just below the head and one on either side of the thorax, Fisher could see heat ripples. Those must be main power intersections. It was remarkable that their bodies could generate that kind of power for long periods.

Alex and Fisher walked side by side. Alex held the chip in his hands, and the newly polished device reflected the sun brightly as noon approached.

They stopped a few paces from the Mechastaceans, who stirred, rotating their strange, bug-like heads. Their camera eyes autofocused.

"The Gemini agreed to the deal," Fisher said. "They asked us to deliver the chip to you out of concern for their safety."

"And was it you who convinced the Gemini to relinquish

control of our precious central operations chip?" said one of them.

"Yes," Fisher said. "We persuaded them. Well, threatened, really." Fisher hoped that their willingness to incur the wrath of the Gemini in order to return the chip would buy them some goodwill.

"But that's our problem," Alex said. "We kept our end of the deal. Now we expect you to keep yours."

The Mechastaceans buzzed and clicked quietly for a moment.

"Once we confirm that is the correct chip, we can guarantee that the Earth's surface will not be destroyed," said the second pirate.

Alex looked sideways at Fisher, hope gleaming from his eyes. *Fate of the world, fate of the world, fate of the world . . .*

Fisher nodded. Alex stepped forward to the Mechastaceans and held out the chip. One of them reached up with a single segmented claw arm and took it. Three small indicator lights on its arm lit up white, and one by one shifted to blue. There was silence for a few moments. Only the flutter of the helicopter blades broke it up. The armed men shifted uneasily, some glancing at Mason, waiting for orders.

"It is authentic," the pirate said. "We thank you for your efforts."

"I'm glad we could come to an agreement," Fisher said,

feeling like a thousand-year glacier had just melted from his back.

"Quite so," the pirate replied. "Diplomacy is the mark of an advanced species."

The Mechastaceans remained in place. Fisher and Alex looked at each other. Was there something they were waiting for? A ritual farewell?

"So . . . that's it?" Fisher said. "Do we say good-bye now?"

The Mechastaceans' metal scales clicked. The resulting noise sounded almost like laughter.

"We are merely taking a moment to admire your world," the Mechastacean leader said. "We believe it will make an excellent base for our operations in this part of the galaxy."

Fisher felt like a sledgehammer had swung down out of the sky right into his stomach.

"A *what*?" he said. Mason had his right hand inside his jacket, and the color had drained from Mr. and Mrs. Bas. The tactical teams pitched their rifles a little higher.

"We want to expand our pirating into this part of the galaxy, and have been looking for a base to operate from. A place where ships can be repaired, and where more of us can be built. We were pursuing the Gemini for the theft of this chip when we happened across your water-filled, mineral-rich world. It was a stroke of luck. Now we will systematically convert your major land masses into factories and repair facilities."

Fisher's fear, anger, and confusion were having a vicious battle for control of his mind. All his life he'd dreamed of enlightened, advanced species visiting humanity and bringing wondrous technology and the knowledge of true peace and happiness. He thought that aliens would help them achieve a world free of disease, poverty, war, and crime. A world where everyone had what they needed.

Instead, it turned out that aliens were just like people. Self-interested, power-grabbing, and opportunistic. They cheated, lied, exploited, and used others to secure their own power base and keep the money flowing. Maybe there were still benevolent, enlightened aliens out there. But as with benevolent, enlightened people, it seemed like they were the exception rather than the rule.

"But the chip—" Alex stuttered through gritted teeth. "You promised—"

"This chip is identical to the one powering our home world's Mother Machine, but not the same one," one Mechastacean said. "This will operate the *new* Mother Machine."

"And what happens to us?" Fisher said.

"It is difficult to say," another Mechastacean said. "Perhaps, in those few regions of the planet we do not require for our use, you may eke out an existence of sorts."

Alex sprang forward, grabbing for the chip, but

the pirate brushed him aside easily and Alex hit the ground hard.

A hot spike of rage shot through Fisher. He and Alex had risked a lot to get the chip back from the Gemini, and now they'd been betrayed. Fisher lunged at the pirate, hoping to catch it off balance. It moved faster than he'd expected, and swatted him off his feet with a long steel arm. Both pirates retreated back toward their shuttle. Fisher landed on his back, the wind completely knocked out of him.

The tactical teams took aim.

"Hold fire!" Mason said. "Hold fire! The boys are too close. *Boys*, get behind me!" Fisher and Alex scrambled out of the way as Mason pulled out a weapon that was definitely about a hundred years ahead of standard FBI issue. Amanda and Veronica jumped from the car as Fisher and Alex reached their parents. Fisher tripped on the turf and crashed to the ground, scraping his forearms and tasting cold earth.

"Wait for my order," Mason said to the men. He turned his focus back to the Mechastaceans. "Listen to me," he said, finger tensed around the trigger, "I am a very good shot. I might not be able to hurt you, but I *can* hit the chip before you get away." Veronica and Mr. Bas helped Fisher to his feet.

The Mechastaceans paused. A long series of nearly

indistinguishable digital static noises emanated from both of them. Mason raised one hand up to keep the weird sounds from rattling his men.

"Ordinarily," the leader said, "you would be correct. But we are already inside the range of our craft's force field." To illustrate the point, a semitransparent white dome became momentarily visible.

"Nevertheless," another Mechastacean said, "your bravery is impressive. So we are prepared to offer you another deal. We will select another rocky world in this system— the next planet out, perhaps." *Mars,* Fisher thought. *Well, people have imagined that there are aliens on Mars for centuries. Wouldn't be so much of a stretch.* "If you provide us with a fee. In order to build our machines, we require certain uncommon metals. Particularly, those of proton counts twenty-two, twenty-nine, forty-six, seventy-four, and seventy-nine."

Mason cocked his head to the side. Amanda and Veronica looked at Fisher and Alex.

"Titanium," Fisher said.

"Copper," Alex said.

"Palladium," Mr. Bas said.

"Tungsten," Mrs. Bas said.

"And gold," Fisher concluded.

"All right," Mason said warily. "How much?"

"All of it," said one pirate.

"What, our entire reserve?" Mason said. "Fort Knox? Everything we've got in our warehouses and factories?"

"No," the other pirate said. "*All* of it."

Fisher's already heavy heart turned to an anchor.

"You're telling me you want all of the gold that has ever been mined," said Mason, finger still tight on the trigger.

"And even the gold that has not," said the Mechastacean. "You have until six P.M., local time. Farewell, and have a pleasant afternoon."

"FIRE!" Mason barked without hesitation, cutting loose with his experimental weapon, which spat crackling white bolts at the chip. His men opened up, and Fisher was deafened by the percussive blasts. Veronica grabbed his arm and pulled him around the back of the car as his parents grabbed Alex. He braced himself for the return fire from the aliens, but it never came. Every shot, even the high-powered bursts from the Apaches' nose cannons, was absorbed harmlessly into the shield, and the Mechastaceans boarded their craft. With a dull roar and a massive gust of air, it lifted off.

The next moment, the shuttle accelerated and was gone.

And so, it seemed, was the last chance for the human race.

≋ CHAPTER 21 ≋

Another day, another potential human extinction. This is why I need a hearty breakfast.

—Vic Daring, Issue #4

Nobody spoke on the short ride back to the underground base. The helicopters flew low above them, and the sound of roaring engines would have drowned out any attempt at conversation, anyway.

Fisher's mind was caught in a series of tight loops of calculation. But he couldn't see any way around the facts.

Earth was done for.

Fisher watched more military vehicles and emplacements move into position in fields and on hillsides, and wondered how long they could possibly hold out. A few days? A week? Would the Mechastaceans pick them off slowly, town by town, or incinerate every city at once? He pictured every single city on Earth in flames. He wondered whether something he could have done would've spared them.

Strangely, he didn't feel much of anything at all. Just kind of cold, and kind of hollow, and weary near the point of collapse. Fisher and Alex had saved the world from one terrible fate only to deliver it straight into another.

Alex and Amanda sat silently, his arm around her shoulders, their heads leaning together. Fisher's dad leaned forward to place his hand on the back of Fisher's mom's seat. Veronica was squeezing Fisher's fingers tightly in hers.

This was all they had, these precious final moments, before the world ended.

Mason was frantically trying to get through to the White House. Fisher couldn't hear what he was saying, but he knew it wouldn't matter, anyway. Unless the president was a time-traveling wizard, what the Mechastaceans had asked for was simply not physically possible.

The whole world was wired with copper. You'd have to rip apart pretty much every electrical grid, house, and machine on Earth to retrieve all the copper humans had unearthed. To do the same for gold, titanium, and the others . . .

Fisher wondered if the Mechastaceans vastly overestimated human physical capacity and work rate . . . or if the whole thing was just a game to them, a sick joke.

Fisher thought about the way that he, and all of them, had been used, and the hollowness and coldness started to give way to something new. A little flame clicked on. It wasn't much. A pilot light. But it grew brighter and hotter.

He'd been pulled back and forth between two alien races competing to take over the planet. He'd been used, tricked, conned. He and his friends were the pieces in a chess game whose players were about to knock the board right off the table. The fire filled up his gut and blossomed into his chest. He wasn't going to be played with anymore.

If he couldn't stop the end from coming, he was at least going to bring some alien invaders down with him.

The guards at the base barely got the gate open in time for the black SUV to barrel its way through.

"Any ideas?" Mason said as they all disembarked.

Fisher turned to him, still feeling that fire burning deep inside of him. "They're not leaving us with any options at this point. I say we fight."

"Seconded," said Amanda.

Alex impatiently hummed a few bars of "Gift-Wrapped Heart," and the door in the silo materialized and slid silently open. The group got into the big steel elevator and started to descend into the base.

"We have to be smart about a counterattack," Mrs. Bas said. "The Mechastaceans are much too strong to take on head-to-head."

The elevator door opened into the cavernous base. Fisher gasped when he looked down to the cave floor. The

Gemini ship was aglow with shifting, flowing lights. A steady, strong rhythm carried all the way up to the top of the cavern. A hatch was open in its side.

The ship was operational.

Fisher bolted for the nearest stairs, everyone else hot on his heels. He clattered down each section of metal steps quicker than the last, knowing but not caring that a wrong slip could send him plummeting to the cave floor.

On the cave floor, the engine thrum was much stronger. Fisher felt it in his bones. His sternum buzzed with every beat of the alien machine's cycle.

Dr. X appeared in the hatchway, a very pleased look on his face. He slowly descended the steps, raising his arms high to indicate the machine around him, as if the group might have failed to notice it.

"From me to you," he said. "A fully functioning extraterrestrial spacecraft, completely under our control."

"Having control of the Gemini ship might change everything," Veronica said excitedly. "We can get close to the pirates. To sneak aboard their ship and attack them when they least expect it."

"Oh," Dr. X said, clasping his hands behind his back. "There is one other thing."

A figure appeared in the hatchway behind him. Short, but imposing. Calm, but arrogant. His hands were clasped

GEMINI SHIP
OPERATIONAL!

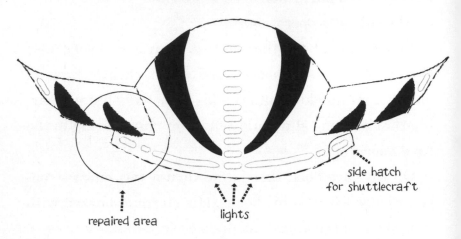

repaired area   lights   side hatch for shuttlecraft

behind his back in much the same way as Dr. X's.

Fisher stumbled backward, gasping. He couldn't believe it.

"Three," Fisher croaked.

Amanda dropped into a wrestling stance. Alex raised his fists into a boxing guard. Even Veronica looked ready to brawl.

Mason pulled out his strange pistol, flicked a switch on its side, and took aim.

"This is set to stun now," he said, "but I promise, it still hurts. A lot. So, Doc, I recommend you start talking before I demonstrate exactly how much 'a lot' is."

Only then did Fisher notice his parents gaping at

Three. Mr. and Mrs. Bas had never gotten a good look at Fisher's second clone during his attempted takeover of Palo Alto. Maybe they'd realized what Three was, and maybe not. Either way, coming face-to-face with another carbon copy of their only son—an evil carbon copy, at that—must have been super creepy.

"Easy now," Dr. X said, raising his hands in a conciliatory gesture. Three stood motionless, a very slim smile on his cold features. "Allow me to explain. I have had a great deal of time and resources at my disposal. In between figuring out how to bring this ship back to life—you're welcome, by the way—I was able to figure out the location of our friend here. With a very small amount of recovered Gemini residue for its rapid shape-changing ability and a sample of Fisher's DNA, I was able to construct a duplicate Three. Not another clone, mind you. It was more or less a statue that appears to breathe—convincing enough, however, to slip into Three's cell when I sent a couple of robots to retrieve him, thanks to the amazing technology on hand here."

"Wait," Fisher said. "A sample of my DNA? How did you get that?"

"A micro-abrasive and adhesive pad stuck to my palm," said Dr. X, holding his hand up. "You did the rest."

Fisher's memory jumped back to what had seemed a weird but totally unimportant moment at the time. The moment played in super slow motion in his head, Dr. X shouting, in a crawling, low-pitched tone, *Hiiiiigggghhh fiiiiiiiive,* as he put up his hand.

"I knew I should've left you hanging," Fisher said bitterly.

"But he betrayed you," Alex said. "Why would you help him?"

"Because he can help us," Dr. X said. "He's brilliant, clever, ruthless, and concerned above all with his own survival. As a threat to his survival, the Mechastaceans are as much his enemy as ours."

Three still hadn't moved. Fisher couldn't bring himself to make eye contact with his shadowy, destructive reflection. No matter *what* the circumstances, Three was a threat to *everyone.* He was an agent of destruction, pure and simple. Just like that, a dousing bucket of water had been tossed onto Fisher's building rage. He felt nothing but fear and confusion.

Three spoke up at last. "As I understand it, the Earth is about to be completely overrun by a hostile, vastly more powerful force." His voice was like Fisher's, if Fisher were hooked up to a huge iron machine that drained from him all traces of feeling. "If we allow the conflict to become open war between the aliens and the nations of Earth, millions will perish in the cross fire, and humanity will lose. What few survive the war will be slaughtered as the

Mechastaceans take over the planet. Human civilization will be completely eradicated. The planet will become a giant manufacturing facility." He inclined his head slightly to the left. "I would likely not survive the conflict, and if I did, life afterward would be very dull."

Three had stepped forward as he spoke. In build and facial structure, he was identical to Fisher and Alex. His hair was dyed black and slicked straight back, and he wore his gray prison jumpsuit like a major general's uniform. His eyes were the same as Fisher's on the surface, but there was no light beneath them. Only an unyielding, stony wall.

"If you have any hope of success," Three said, "you'll need to enlist help not just from your friends, but from your enemies, too."

"What do you mean?" said Amanda, scowling.

"Even the combined armies of every industrialized nation on Earth won't be able to defeat the Mechastaceans head-on, which means you must be planning an infiltration," said Three. "Trying to slip into their fleet on a Gemini spacecraft will be difficult no matter what, but it will be impossible if you do not first distract them with an attack elsewhere. Using your own military forces will cost human lives unnecessarily. Why not distract them with a powerful force, a race with whom they are already at war."

"The Gemini," said Alex slowly.

"He's right," Veronica said with a look like she'd just downed a grass-clippings-and-library-dust milk shake. "If we want to slip past the Mechastaceans' defenses, we need their attention elsewhere. We need a diversion, and a big one."

Agent Mason looked to Fisher, raising his eyebrows inquiringly.

"I agree with Three." Fisher forced the words out. "The Gemini have the power, and the motive, to go after the Mechastaceans."

Mason holstered his weapon.

"Because the planet is at stake, I will allow your help, if you cooperate fully and agree to constant supervision," Mason said, addressing Three. "If you double-cross us, I'll toss you in a cell the size of a phone booth until the sun burns out or I have a change of heart. Which I will not."

For a few seconds, Three stayed motionless. Then the right corner of his mouth curled up very slightly, and he inclined his head.

"We have a deal then," he said. "I will help you defeat the Mechastaceans."

But Fisher was far from reassured. Had they given humanity a fighting chance?

Or doomed it to total extinction?

CHAPTER 22

More than 99% of all species that have ever existed are extinct. I never have been one to follow trends.

—Alex Bas, Personal Notes

Fisher knocked on the door of the Gemini's bus for what he hoped would be the last time. Anna and Bee opened the door and broke into identical scowls.

"What do you want?" Anna said.

"Your help, believe it or not," said Fisher. "Turns out, pirates are not men of their words. Or . . . lobsters of their words. Whatever. The point is, they're planning to take over the Earth. We're going to stop them, but we can't do it without you."

"Why should we help you?" Bee said.

"Because if you do, you get your ship back," Fisher said. "Packed with explosives, of course, so that we can detonate it at a moment's notice if you turn on us again. Also, the navigation computer will be locked on a one-way trip back to your home planet."

Anna's and Bee's eyes flickered.

"Perhaps we could . . . *unite* against our common foe," Bee said. "In the interest of our survival and yours.

What exactly would you have us do?"

"The Mechastacean scout ship has landed in the Mojave Desert," Fisher said. "We're going to fly your ship straight into their fleet. You will attack the grounded scout ship. Hopefully, the attack will dominate their attention and resources, so they won't notice us sneaking in by space."

The Gemini drones stood completely still. Fisher knew that their mind must be pondering the suggested truce. He held his breath.

"We have one stipulation," Bee said finally.

"All right," Fisher said carefully. "What?"

"We want a large stock of the seeds from which your 'potatoes' grow," said Anna. "And instructions for converting them into several-pointed crispy eatables."

It took Fisher a moment to work out what she meant by *several-pointed crispy eatables*. "You . . . want to make your own spicy star fries?" Fisher said, struggling not to laugh when Anna and Bee nodded. "Fine. We'll give you as many seeds as you can carry and the recipe."

For the first time in a long time, Anna and Bee smiled.

"We will tell you a secret," Anna said. "The Mechastaceans are almost entirely mechanical," Anna said. "But their flagship has a very small organic core. We do not know where in the ship it is, but if you remove or destroy it, the entire fleet will be disabled."

"Thank you," Fisher said sincerely. "We'll do our best."

He had a feeling the Gemini still couldn't be trusted, but he literally didn't have time to worry about that right now. He handed Bee a little phone that Agent Mason had given to him, which sent and received special encrypted signals to the MORONS communication system. "You'll hear from us when we know exactly when we want you to strike."

He turned away without another word and jogged down the steps and into his house. There were three more elements crucial to the mission: Whatever gear Fisher could scrounge from his bedroom lab, the hacking and calculating prowess of his AI, CURTIS, and the most potent, least predictable force in the known world: Flying Pig.

≋ CHAPTER 23 ≋

Space. My favorite one-word sentence.

—Alex Bas, Journal

FP took one look at the MORONS cavern, sped away from Fisher, and joyfully leapt off the catwalk, spreading his tiny wings and spiraling down through the air toward the Gemini ship.

"I can see how he might come in handy," Agent Mason said, straightening his black tie.

"In more ways than you'd expect," Fisher answered, watching the little pink dot descend lower and lower until he reached the floor with an ungainly thump.

Fisher carried a big backpack filled with whatever equipment had caught his eye in a very quick dash through his house. He also had a portable hard drive slung around his neck on a chain in which CURTIS was riding. The powerful AI would be the key to finding their way through the Mechastacean flagship and determining where the organic core was—if such a thing did, indeed, exist.

The whole base was buzzing with more agents, special ops soldiers, scientists, and engineers than Fisher had ever seen. Announcements rang out from the loudspeaker system at least three times a minute, messages flashed across giant display screens, and hundreds of technicians swarmed across the ship, checking every centimeter for leaks, cracks, structural weaknesses, and any other crash damage that the repair teams might have missed.

By the time Fisher got to the ground floor, all of the shouting voices and clanging machinery had fused into a roar. A massive screen showing radar reports had been installed against one wall of the cave. On one side of its display was a big circle he took to be Earth. Nearly two dozen objects were approaching. The first of them had just passed inside the Moon's orbit.

The alien fleet was arriving.

Alex emerged from the mass of scientists, holding FP in his arms.

"They're coming," Alex said, pointing up at the big screen. "Mason's gathering everyone near the ship for a mission briefing," Alex said. "You ready?"

"As ready as I'll ever be," Fisher said, scratching FP behind the ears.

"So . . . that's a no?" Alex said with a faint smile.

Fisher managed to smile, too. "Exactly. But what else can we do?"

"Nothin' at all," Alex said as FP snout-nuzzled his chin. "Shall we?"

"Let's," Fisher said, jogging his backpack higher.

Mason stood with his back to the ship, a slender tablet arranged on a podium in front of him. Fisher, Alex, their parents, Amanda, and Veronica took seats in front of him. FP sat in Fisher's arms. Dr. X and Three stood off to the side—surrounded, Fisher couldn't help but notice with a certain grim satisfaction, by armed guards. Clearly, Mason wasn't taking any chances.

"Here's the situation," Mason said. He swiped the tablet and a hologram popped into existence above it. The Earth was in the center, with the Moon's orbit shown as a glowing line. The pirate fleet was displayed in full detail.

"The remainder of the Mechastacean fleet has been approaching rapidly for the past day," Mason said. "They'll reach low orbit in a matter of hours. When they do, they're going to demand our immediate surrender, and we will refuse. That will trigger the largest war in human history. It will also very likely be the last *event* in human history."

Fisher watched everyone's face turn grim and stony. Only Three's expression remained as unnervingly curious as always. People were a source of amusement to him, only useful to him as stepping-stones. The evil clone looked like he was taking in the human exhibit at the zoo. The way things were going, the zoo might be the only spot humans existed in the future.

"Don't get me wrong," Mason said, "I'd rather go out

with a furious fight for our lives than surrender. But it would be best to avoid both options."

He tapped his screen and the hologram zoomed in on one of the ships. Most of the Mechastaceans' ships were variations on the scout ship's design: blocky, sharp-angled, basically rectangles in space, albeit huge and terrifying ones.

But this ship was different. It was much bigger than the others, and shaped like a capital *C* with sharpened ends.

"This is their flagship," said Mason, pausing to take a breath as everyone marveled at its size. "It's at least five miles port to starboard, maybe more bow to stern. It's tough to get an exact reading. According to what the Gemini said"—he nodded to indicate Fisher—"this ship is the key to the whole fleet's operation. Take out its core, and the fleet falls apart. Let's hope they were telling the truth." He paused and tapped another button on the screen. Now the hologram showed an image of the scout ship, grounded in the middle of the Mojave Desert. "In less than an hour," he resumed, "the Gemini will launch their assault. Our helicopters will drop them off nearby and then make like crazy for a safe distance. They're back up to twenty-six, and with their powers of transformation and explosion, they can certainly give the scout ship a good fight."

"And while that's happening, we're going up to the

pirate flagship to disable it," Amanda said eagerly.

"That's right," Mason said coolly. "You four"—he indicated the kids—"have more experience with alien contact than anyone on Earth, and you've proven yourselves capable of handling infiltration. You'll be our field agents. The Bas parents, Dr. X, and I will direct the mission from here. Fisher and Veronica, you're in charge of logistics and tactics. Amanda, you're the muscle." Amanda gave a rare smile. "To that end, I've got something that will even the playing field should you have to go up against the Mechastaceans in one-on-one combat."

He held up a suit made of thin-looking black fabric with sleek silver trim.

"Fisher told us all about his strength-enhancing sleeves, and their use during an unfortunate dodgeball incident," Mason said, barely concealing a smile. "He was good enough to give us two to reverse engineer. Our people had just enough time to manufacture this full-body suit." He tossed the suit to Amanda, who caught it one-handed. "Which brings us to Alex," Mason went on. "You're the pilot."

"The pilot?" Alex said, eyes practically popping. "I can't even drive a *car*. How am I supposed to fly an alien spacecraft?"

"With this," Mason said, holding up a glass of water. "Your mother's H2Info. Everything we've learned about how the Gemini ship works is in here, along with the training of a fighter pilot."

He handed it to Alex, who looked at it, shrugged, and drained the glass in a single gulp.

"And me?" Three said, turning his reptilian gaze to Mason.

"Your capacity for violence and mayhem is astounding," said Mason. "As much as I'd prefer to have you padlocked in a door-less cell, we may very well need both violence and mayhem in spades." He frowned. "You're the emergency device. The bomb we set off if things start going wrong. You will be restrained in a full-body manacle to which Fisher has the only release. Fisher, you will decide when, and if, you need him."

Fisher could feel the clone's gaze slip across him like sharkskin, and he couldn't help but shiver. He now held the key to unleash one of the most destructive forces ever created. It was bad enough that they were relying on the Gemini to give them the opening they'd need to carry out their mission. Adding Three into the mix made it a far more volatile one. He swore that he'd keep Three locked up until there was truly no other choice.

"I won't lie," Mason said, scratching the back of his neck and looking down at the floor with the expression of a person who long ago passed the point of desperation. "Ordinarily, we'd plan and train for a mission like this for months. A year, if possible. This is a longshot. It's also the only shot. So man your ship, and may the . . . well, you know." He smiled.

Fisher and Alex got up and instantly had half the life crushed out of them by their parents.

"Come back to us," Mr. Bas managed to choke out.

"And if you can save the world while you're at it, that would be great," Mrs. Bas half sobbed.

"Mmpphh," Fisher said, wriggling away from his parents' death grip. "We'll be fine," he said, trying to sound reassuring. "Back before you know it."

"With the world saved and everything," Alex said, forcing a grin.

Amanda and Veronica had stepped away for a moment and Fisher had to look around to spot them. They were being crushed in the arms of their own parents. When they returned, Fisher smiled at Veronica.

"How in the world did you get them to agree to this?" he said.

"I took care of that," said Mason. "Or, more accurately, I called the president, and he took care of it. Their parents received calls from him personally. It took a little convincing, but now that they know what's going on, they gave their permission."

"I'm sure it took more than a little convincing, even from the president," Veronica said, chuckling and waving back at her parents. "Not all parents are as cool as yours."

"You hear that?" Alex said. "You two are cool! Up top!" He put up his hand for a high five. Mr. Bas sort of pushed his palm into Alex's with a goofy smile.

They suited up. Amanda put on the strength suit, and flexed her arms with satisfaction. Fisher had brought his well-tested spy suits for himself, FP, and Alex, along with a new one for Veronica. In their sleek, black jumpsuits they certainly looked the part of heroes. Fisher wished they could've taken the ChameleoClothes to sneak in, but those had mini-generators and used a considerable amount of power. No matter what they looked like, the power signatures would be easy to track inside the pirate flagship. Fisher picked up his gear bag with one hand and his spy-suited pig with the other.

There was nothing else to do but board the ship. The inside was awash with shifting, flowing colors, like a million tie-dyed shirts in a whirlpool. The colors flowed across the walls, under their feet, and over their heads.

"Wow," Fisher said. "What is all this?"

"Well," Alex said, pointing to a flowing green line dotted with lavender splotches, "that's the power usage meter. And that orange ball hopping around is the cooling system readout. The aliens that designed this ship before the Gemini stole it don't visually express language with writing, but with color patterns. I can't read

BATTLE PLAN TO DEFEAT THE MECHASTACEANS AND SAVE PLANET EARTH AND THE HUMAN RACE FROM DESTRUCTION:

1. Fly Gemini ship to outer space.
2. Focus on the mission and not how cool space is.
3. Infiltrate Mechastacean mothership.
4. Destroy the ship's core.
5. Don't die? Victory?

Weeeeeee

it all . . . there's only so much they were able to encode in the H2Info, I guess . . . but I've got a pretty good idea of what most of it means."

Padded seats had been installed by the MORONS team. Fisher settled into his position and buckled himself in, watching the wild colors jump over his head. Alex sat in front of a pair of flat panels, which he set his arms onto, nodding that he understood how the controls worked. Fisher buckled FP to the side of his own harness.

Mason wheeled in Three on a hand truck. The clone had restraints at his wrists, elbows, knees, and ankles. He clipped the restraints into a pair of hooks set into the wall, and handed Fisher a tiny remote with a single button on a chain.

"Only if you need him," Mason said.

"You can be sure of that," Fisher said, slipping the chain around his neck, where it settled next to his portable hard drive.

"Okay, people," Mason said. "Get the job done, and get home. That's all there is to it."

"Yes, sir," Amanda said, nodding.

"You got it," Alex said. Mason left, and a minute later they heard the airlock shut behind him. This was it. Once they were in space, nobody would be able to help them. Nobody would be able to rescue them if things went badly.

Fisher had a sudden idea, and he hefted the Three

remote in his palm, took a miniature tool kit from his spy suit, and popped it open.

"What are you doing?" said Three in his normal chilly tone.

"Boosting the range," Fisher said, unbuckling himself, taking a few cautious steps toward Three to adjust the little receiver on his restrains. Three's perfectly even, calm breathing ruffled Fisher's hair, and Fisher felt as if spiders were creeping down his back. "It's . . . a big ship."

"Hmm," Three said, raising an eyebrow. Fisher tinkered with the transmitter and the receiver for another minute, then hastily returned to his seat, wishing he could shower.

"*Perseus,* this is control," Mason's voice came in over the ship's comm system.

"Is that us?" Fisher said.

"My idea," Veronica said. "The hero who braved unspeakable dangers to enter Medusa's dark lair."

"This is *Perseus,*" Alex said. "Ready when you are, control."

"The Gemini have begun their attack on the Mechastacean scout ship," Mason said. "You're clear to launch, repeat, clear to launch."

"Hey," Fisher said, "how exactly do we launch, anyway?"

"Right now," Alex said, "the top of this silo is opening like a convertible roof. Get ready, everyone."

The low thumping of the engine became louder and higher pitched. Alex made a quick swipe at the controls and the front of the room became a screen, displaying the view in front of them. Only when Fisher saw the cave wall sliding *downward* did he realize they were already in the air. The ship must have a system to compensate for g-forces, necessary since they'd be accelerating to very high speeds.

Daylight became visible, and then they were in the open air, hovering just above the base.

"Here we go . . . " Alex said.

With a single twitch of Alex's right hand, the *Perseus* shot across the sky like a cannonball. The ground became a greenish-brownish blur, clouds turned to white flashes in the sky, and Fisher could feel the ship rushing through the air. In seconds, the blue sky turned to navy, then to black, and the stars popped into brilliance.

They were in space.

⇛ CHAPTER 24 ⇚

WE WERE BORN OF THE STARS. EVERY ATOM IN OUR BODIES HEAVIER THAN HYDROGEN WAS CREATED IN A STAR. AND AS WITH ANY PARENTS, I'M SURE THEY'D APPRECIATE A VISIT.

—WALTER BAS, SPEECH EXCERPT

Fisher's body bounced a little against his restraints as the *Perseus* freed itself from Earth's gravity well and free fall set in. Stress and tension left his joints as his weight disappeared.

The girls' hair drifted like seaweed, and FP flailed his legs in the air as he floated up on the tether connecting his spy suit to Fisher's chair. He squealed happily as he spun himself.

"*Wow,*" Alex said. "Fisher, we've got to get one of these."

Fisher couldn't respond. He was speechless, gazing out across the stars. This was what he'd spent his whole life dreaming about. Sailing the void, skimming the edge of human advancement, and helping to guide civilization to its future. Or in this case, making sure that it had one.

"This is wild," Amanda said, watching her hair drift around her face.

"I just wish we had more time to enjoy it," Fisher said,

reaching out to give FP a little push to help his spin.

"We're approaching the pirate fleet," Alex said. "This thing has a stealth system, but it can only help us so much. Let's hope the Gemini have their attention . . . Control, do you copy?

"This is control," Mason's voice replied. "You'll reach the edge of the pirate fleet in under one minute. One of their frigates should be directly ahead. Accelerate to seventy percent speed and stay as close to its hull as you can to avoid its scans."

Dots that had looked like tiny stars became bigger and brighter. Moments later, the fleet was all around them, crowding out the sky. As Mason had said, one of the Mechastacean ships was dead ahead, and their weight briefly returned as Alex accelerated toward it.

"Hang on," Alex said, and flipped the *Perseus* up and over the black and red hull of the colossal warship, skimming along its surface. A jutting weapon emplacement appeared right in their path. Alex executed a swift juke and Fisher clutched his seat as they missed it by less than a meter. A second later the vast vessel was left behind.

"Looks like somebody's spotted us," Alex said. "Fisher, could you scramble their comms for me?"

"Um, how?" Fisher said.

"With this jamming system," Alex said smoothly. Fisher marveled at his mother's H2Info, and wished he'd drunk from a glass of water encoded with information called *How to save Earth from imminent alien destruction*. "It'll spit out a blast of radio interference that should overload its system for a few minutes." A cable extended from the ceiling toward Fisher. The end unfolded into a screen that displayed the ships around them as gray dots. One of the dots turned bright white. It was following them.

Fisher didn't need any further instructions. He grabbed the joystick, centered it so that a small crosshair lined up with the pursuing craft, and pressed the red button. The ship vibrated slightly. The pursuing ship slowed down, then peeled away.

"Nice shot!" Alex said. "Their sensors and comms are down. They'll need to reboot before they can come after us again. By that time we should be aboard the flagship. Speaking of which . . . "

Fisher looked up at the main screen.

"Look at the size of that thing," Amanda said, her jaw dropping open.

Even at this distance the flagship was too big for them to make out its shape. In seconds it had filled the whole screen. It looked like a wall at the end of the universe.

"Does it know we're here?" Veronica asked in a hushed voice.

"I don't think so," said Alex, but he sounded uneasy.

"The *Perseus* has been discreetly scanning it for the past few minutes. I see a few possible entrances. I'm taking us into one of the smaller docking bays. Amanda, if somebody's waiting in there, you'll need to act quickly."

"On it," Amanda said, punching her palm.

An opening appeared in the side of the ship, and the *Perseus* made for it. They slipped soundlessly into the gaping dark mouth, touching down on a loading bay that held several small spacecraft and a number of huge storage tanks set into the walls.

"Bringing us in," Alex said tensely. "Amanda, there are two Mechastaceans in the bay, and they're coming toward us. If you could get over to the airlock, please?"

Amanda released her restraints and disappeared into the corridor.

"We're inside!" Alex said. Two Mechastaceans were now visible on the main screen, walking right up to where the ship was about to land. A dark shape flew in from off camera and landed on one of the aliens. After a second Fisher realized it was Amanda.

She moved so fast his eyes could barely follow. She leapt onto one alien, fists flying. The suit pumped up her strength so much, she could bust pieces of steel carapace into shards with every impact. A final strike went straight through the thing's body and it fell. She hurled herself onto the second alien, and with a single double-handed wrench tore a tangle of cables and wires from its midsection. By the time the ship had powered down completely, both of the robots were on the floor, motionless.

Alex, Fisher, Veronica, and FP disembarked to find Amanda standing over the second pirate with her fists on her hips.

"Well done," Veronica said, kneeling down next to one, running her hand along its exoskeleton curiously.

"Thanks," Amanda said with a triumphant smile. "What about Three?"

"I'm leaving him on the Gemini ship," Fisher said. "I've got the remote with me."

He took a close look at one of the Mechastaceans, examining the busted-up areas that Amanda had created, and reaching in under a hole she'd put near the thing's head. Just as he'd suspected, he felt the thick, insulated cable of heavy power conduits. "Looks like these robots have power line clusters here, here and here," he said, pointing to the two other spots on the pirate's side he'd identified earlier. "Aiming to disable those spots should help."

They surveyed the room cautiously. It didn't seem any alarms had sounded, but Fisher couldn't be sure. A pair of shuttles sat on either side of the bay. There was a single large door opposite the force-field-covered opening to space, and a number of small hatches along the sides. FP sniffed at the floor, then at the inert Mechastaceans.

Veronica opened up Fisher's backpack and distributed radio earpieces to everyone. Almost immediately, their earbuds crackled, indicating a transmission.

"The Gemini have retreated," Agent Mason said in their ears. "Diversion's over."

"Perfect timing," Fisher said. "We're on the flagship."

"Good," Mason said, "get CURTIS set up and go find the core."

"On it," Fisher said.

Fisher walked back into the ship and hooked his portable hard drive to a special port that Dr. X had built onto the *Perseus*'s controls. The hard drive woke up, hummed, and beeped as Fisher's AI was transferred into the ship's memory. "CURTIS, you there?"

"Am I!" the AI said, voice booming from the ship's speakers. "The hardware in this thing is amazing! The kind of processing power I'm working with—"

"Well, we need you to work with it right now," Fisher cut him off. Getting two completely different systems of computer hardware to mesh wasn't a task he envied the team of MORONS programmers and hackers who'd been given it. "Hack in as quietly as you can and find us the central core on this beast, would you?"

"Working!" said CURTIS. "I'm using the *Perseus*'s antenna to access this ship's mainframe. Getting some resistance, hang on . . . " A low hum emanated from the hard drive. Fisher imagined his AI frowning. Every second felt like an eternity. "Got it," CURTIS said at last. "It's a bit of a trip. Go through the middle hatch on the left. I'll talk you there by radio. Make it snappy, okay? I don't know how long I can hang around without getting booted out of their system."

They lined up at the hatch: Amanda first, then Alex, then Veronica, with Fisher bringing up the rear, gear bag slung across his back, FP snorting excitedly at his feet. In one sense, they were lucky the ship was so enormous. There were probably millions of Mechastaceans aboard. Two disabled Mechastaceans might not raise an alarm for quite some time.

"All set?" Amanda said.

"Pop it," said Fisher.

There was a lever in the hatch's center. Amanda pulled it. The hatch clanked but didn't budge. Fisher's heart dropped.

"Locked," Amanda said. "Hang on . . . " She wrapped both hands around the lever, braced her legs against the bulkhead, gritted her teeth, and with a strong exhale, ripped the hatch right out of the wall. Fisher's confidence returned, along with a newfound appreciation for the MORONS engineers and the way they'd improved on his own technology. Amanda set the hatch down neatly on the ground. "Let's go."

"Hold up," Fisher said. "I have a little scout for us." He reached into the gear bag and pulled out a small metal ball. He tapped a button and it unfolded into a hovering robot with a tennis-ball-shaped body and a single arm. It was his pickpocket drone, which he'd initially designed to commandeer his parents' Loopity Land passes—and it was finally getting some use. "I'll send this ahead of us, so we don't get any unpleasant surprises."

The hatch would be small for a Mechastacean, but the four kids slipped through it easily, following the little drone, which buzzed quietly in front of Amanda. They found themselves in a long, black hallway with very low lighting.

"You're in a maintenance corridor," said CURTIS over the radio. "Keep going straight."

The sounds of the ship in operation pattered and rang distantly. The creaks and groans of the immense vessel's structure drifted down the corridor as they walked. Fisher's own breathing got louder in his ears. At any moment, a Mechastacean could emerge from almost anywhere in the darkness ahead. Or maybe they stayed out of here because something even they were afraid of dwelled in the dismal space. It looked just about right for some kind of huge, toothy worm. . . .

Fisher shook his head to clear the primal terror from it. He had plenty of real things to be scared of without his imagination piling on more. He focused on staying alert and moving quietly. Amanda stayed in a crouch, ready to spring. Two minutes later, the drone stopped, hovering low over a spot on the floor. Amanda put her hand up, and they came to a quick halt.

"What is it?" Fisher whispered.

"Something in the floor," Amanda whispered back. "Could be a pressure-sensitive plate."

"Here," Fisher said, handing forward a multi-tool from his bag that was basically an excessively large Swiss Army Knife. It was small, heavy, and expendable, since he had two more just like it.

"Back up a little," Amanda said, and they did as she wound up for an underhand toss. The tool landed on the floor in front of them with a clatter. Instantly, three white beams lanced from one wall to the other, at ankle, waist, and head level. The drone barely avoided them, zipping up toward the ceiling. Fisher could feel the heat from the beams even from the back. The lasers winked out, and they heard a whine as the beams started to recharge.

"Let's mark this spot so we don't accidentally step on it later," Fisher said, giving Amanda a small can of luminescent spray paint. Amanda tiptoed up to the pressure plate and marked it with neon green. They stepped over the plate one by one. Fisher picked up FP and held him carefully to his chest. The tool hadn't been damaged, but

Fisher didn't want to risk disturbing the plate again, and left it where it was. The drone continued buzzing on. No further traps marked the corridor.

"Hold here," said CURTIS in Fisher's earbud. "I'm going to open a hatch in the floor in front of you." The AI was true to his word, and a piece of floor slid aside. "There's a circular room down there. It's a power substation, I think. From it you'll be able to get to an elevator."

"An elevator to what?" Fisher said, looking into the dim blue light glowing up through the hatch.

"Not sure, kid," CURTIS said. "Still working on that. I'm having a harder and harder time dodging their cyber security. If this ship's computer didn't have so many things to do at once, it probably woulda found me already."

Unless, of course, it already *had* found him, and reprogrammed him to guide them all right into a trap. The idea occurred to Fisher suddenly, and he felt his stomach pool into his shoes. Fisher stared at the big hatch. Every decision now meant the difference between life and death.

"Let's send the drone in first," Fisher whispered. The pickpocket drone buzzed down through the hatch.

Instantly, three high-energy beams lanced out and turned the drone to a puff of glittery smoke.

"Now!" Fisher shouted. "Before the lasers recharge!"

Amanda and Alex dropped in, followed by Veronica and Fisher, who gripped FP tightly. The room was lit a deep blue, with control consoles set all along the walls.

Amanda instantly tackled one of the three Mechastaceans manning the controls. FP jumped out of Fisher's arms. Fisher and Alex ran for another. Fisher's fight or flight kicked into full gear as the pirate swung a long claw buzzing with an electric charge at his head, and he ducked and rolled away. The brothers shifted positions. Fisher felt the rush of air as a metal talon slashed right past his face. Veronica leapt into the fight, wielding a pry bar she had grabbed from the gear bag. As Alex and Fisher kept the Mechastacean occupied, she delivered a heavy strike to its left-side weak point. It staggered as the power flow to that side diminished, but still managed a counter-swing with a whirring claw. Fisher pulled Veronica to the ground to get her out of its path.

"Fisher!" Alex shouted. Fisher tossed his brother the pry bar, which Alex caught neatly in one hand. Alex wound up and delivered a strong blow to the power junction below its head. It lurched backward, then toppled over, releasing a shower of sparks.

FP hopped onto it and gave it a few hoofs to the head for good measure.

Fisher turned, panting for breath, his arm muscles burning. He found the two other pirates sparking on the floor, Amanda dusting off her hands. In the blue glow that filled the room, she looked rather like an alien conqueror herself.

"You guys all right?" CURTIS said over the radio.

"Fine, CURTIS," Fisher said, sucking in a deep breath.

"Swell!" the AI said. "I'm patching Agent Mason through to you."

"What's your progress, team?" Mason's voice said a little fuzzily.

"In the belly of the beast, sir," said Fisher, taking Veronica's hand to reassure her, and himself. "CURTIS is navigating us through the ship. I think we're getting close."

"That's good," Mason said, "because things are getting antsy down here. The fact that the Mechastaceans aren't responding is putting a lot of countries in the mood to strike first, and strike hard."

"How hard?" Alex said.

"Nuclear hard," Mason said. Fisher and Alex looked at one another, eyes wide. "There's mounting pressure to throw everything we have at them. If they're too close to the Earth when a barrage like that hits . . . "

"The magnetosphere won't stop all the radiation," Fisher said quietly. "And any ships that get knocked out will fall to Earth as meteors." He took a deep breath. "Okay, the clock just got shorter. We'll check in again when we can. Out." There was a click as the connection with Mason ended. "CURTIS?"

"Right with ya," CURTIS said. "Look for a red panel on the wall. It should have up and down arrows, like an elevator. You want to go down as far as you can."

"Found it," Veronica said. The red panel had faint white triangles pointing up and down, and she pressed the down arrow. A door opened next to the panel. Inside the door there was nothing but green light. Veronica hesitated.

"This isn't bad," Fisher said earnestly, taking Veronica's hand. "Alex and I took one yesterday. Shall we?"

They stepped into the green light together. Once again, they were immediately weightless. Fisher let FP flap around them gleefully as all together they drifted downward. They passed through the largest open space any of them had ever seen. Fisher nearly hyperventilated at the sensation of hurtling through vast emptiness. In spite of the physical comfort of gently drifting down, the sight made him extremely dizzy.

Other, parallel transport beams filled the colossal chamber. Thousands of them. Some of them held traveling Mechastaceans, others had cargo.

"Fisher," Alex said, "somebody's gonna see us."

"Not to worry," said Fisher, reaching into his backpack. He removed the latest in his long series of disguises, crate-in-a-box. A name that, while not very creative, was certainly better than its prototype name, "box-within-a-larger-box."

The dark plastic cube fit in his palm. He tapped the top twice, and it opened. Then the flat pieces that had opened unfolded again, doubling in size. The little device repeated the process until it became a seven-foot cube with one open side. They huddled together. Fisher raised the weightless crate over their heads, then pulled it down over them.

"Now we're just another cargo load," he said. The inside of the box was lit up green from the beam beneath them.

Something was coming up toward them. Or more accurately, they were moving down toward *it*. At first it was a dark smudge, then it resolved into an opening just wide enough to accommodate the beam.

"Heads up," Amanda said a minute later. "About to go into somewhere."

Fisher pulled the crate off of them and collapsed it again as they passed into a tunnel. Their feet touched ground at last, and the beam switched off. They were in a rectangular room with flat, featureless walls.

"CURTIS, where are we?" Fisher said.

"You're on the right level, kid," CURTIS said. "Main engineering, I think. The maps I've found are a little unclear, but there should be . . . oh, uh, hang on. Something's happening."

Fisher looked from one wall to another. *Something happening* was almost never good news.

BLUEPRINTS FOR
CRATE-IN-A-BOX

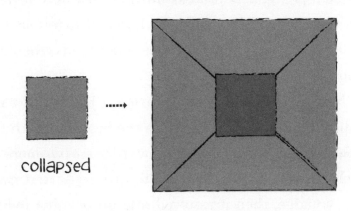

collapsed

deployed

Did this really
need blueprints?

SERIOUSLY ALEX
STOP READING
MY LAB NOTES!!!

"What?" Alex said, fear creeping into his voice, "What does that mean?"

Suddenly, the walls fell away. Like flats in a movie set, they simply dropped. The room they were actually in was immense, and it was full of Mechastaceans. Behind the wall of steel bodies was a pedestal with a series of cables snaking from it. On top of the pedestal was an object about the size of a basketball that looked like a cross between a brain and a cactus.

Fisher felt a surge of excitement, followed immediately by the heavy pull of despair. So the Gemini were right. There *was* an organic core. But there were at least fifty heavily armed space pirates between them and it.

"Welcome, humans," said one of the pirates, stepping forward. Its metal shell was red and gold, and silver stars decorated its upper segments. "You arrived even more quickly than we expected."

The pirates took a step in. The four circled up, backs together. FP snarled in his odd pig fashion. Amanda growled low in her throat.

"Fisher?" Mason's voice crackled in his ear. "What's going on? Anyone read me?"

"This was a trap all along," Veronica whispered.

"Yes," the leader said. "It was natural to expect you to make an attempt against our flagship's core, knowing that you were in contact with the Gemini, who might disclose to you our only true weakness."

The pirates inched forward again.

"Amanda," Alex said, pulling her into him, preferring a last embrace to an impossible fight. Veronica put her arms on Fisher's shoulders and leaned into him.

"No, no, no . . . " Mason's voice said with desperate breathlessness across the tens of thousands of miles separating them. "I—I'm sorry, everyone."

All hope was lost. Fisher had only one remaining weapon at his disposal—one final hope. One last prayer.

Three.

"No, *I'm* sorry," Fisher said firmly. He pulled the chain holding the remote from his neck. "I really hate to do this."

Before anyone could blink, one of the pirates spat out a pencil-thin particle beam that turned the remote to a cloud of atoms.

"Fool," the leader said. "Haven't you realized yet that you, with your biological reaction times, can't possibly hope to defeat us?"

Tears welled up in Veronica's eyes. Even Alex looked stricken.

Fisher hung his head, closing his eyes. He let out a long sigh. Then he started to laugh—a thin, whispery chuckle that made even Amanda turn and look at him with something like fear in her eyes.

The approaching Mechastaceans hesitated as their leader raised a hand.

"This is your kind's sound for amusement, I believe," it said. "What is amusing you?"

Fisher raised his head, and smiled coldly back at the pirate.

"The transmitter you just destroyed was a dead man switch," he said. "I reprogrammed it to send out a constant signal. Our weapon is deployed when the signal *stops*."

No sooner had he finished speaking than the floor began to shake. Lights began to flash above their heads—a soundless alarm, Fisher figured—and a holographic display popped into place against one wall, showing the exact location and method of the ship's breach.

Three was rampaging along a hallway the size of a city street, cutting down everything he saw with a pair of blazing beam weapons. Wielding weapons that spat blinding blasts and practically dancing as he dodged, ducked, and leapt over returning fire, Three was carving a path through the ship. Fisher couldn't have brought along a better backup plan if he'd bottled an avalanche. It was inspiring, reinvigorating, and absolutely terrifying.

Three turned and blazed a broad path along a series of storage tanks and what looked like power relays along one side of the hall.

A second, much larger explosion rocked the deck, and several of the pirates fell down. The others were thrown into disarray. An alarm screamed overhead, making Fisher's ears ring, and blue lights blazed in the walls. More than half of the pirates paused and tilted their heads, light sequences blinking on their fronts. They must've been receiving a signal. Apparently that signal was an urgent request to assist with the havoc Three was wreaking elsewhere, because they immediately turned and dashed from the room. Fisher turned to look at Alex, then Amanda, then Veronica. As one, they nodded.

Fisher ducked, scooped up FP, and hurled him high into the air, pointing at the core. Now it was their job to make sure FP made it there.

Alex popped a pair of small orbs from one sleeve and nodded to Fisher. Alex raised his arm in a long backward windup like a softball pitcher. As two pirates charged, Alex hurled the orbs underhand. They hit the pirates and popped, releasing twin electrical bursts that blinked like tiny clouds of lightning. The pirates crumpled, systems shorting out, reduced to heaps of inanimate metal.

Amanda grabbed the nearest pirate by its long, segmented tail, set her legs wide, and with a massive heave, threw it into two of its companions. Fisher reached into the bag and tossed Veronica a foot-long tube that immediately extended into a five-foot staff with electric prods at both ends. He took out another for himself, and they charged into the fray.

Their odds were terrible. But with all humanity at stake, there was nothing to do but fight, and hope that probability was looking the other way.

CHAPTER 25

Sometimes, people just tune out your words. But nobody can tune out your actions.

—Amanda Cantrell, Personal Notes

Fisher let fury drive him forward. The Mechastaceans had tricked him into handing them the key to the Earth's demise, and he was going to pay them back in full, or die trying. He swung left as Veronica swung right. He ducked under an attacking claw as she swung her staff up to meet it.

FP glided through the air, and they charged after him, knocking down every Mechastacean that tried to intercept his flight. Amanda dove straight at the closest pirate to her, punching and kicking it until it was in fully five pieces. Two more aliens came at her from both sides, and she drove an elbow straight into one's face before flipping onto the other's back and cracking it almost in half. Alex had drawn a pair of stun batons from his belt and was covering her advance, sweeping up anyone she missed. One Mechastacean nearly struck Amanda down, but Alex executed a flurry of rapid jabs that sent electricity surging through its metal body and left it fluttering on its side.

FP reached the core and grabbed it in his strong jaws. The ship immediately responded to the core's theft. Lights blinked and Fisher felt the deck shifting alarmingly under his feet, as if it had been turned to Jell-O.

"Kiddos!" CURTIS shouted in Fisher's ear at maximum volume to be heard over the din of the fight. Fisher plunged his staff straight up into a pirate's camera eye as CURTIS continued, and the Mechastacean flailed blindly, knocking over one of its comrades. "Don't know what's goin' on down there, but Three is making a mess of the place, and the central computer is going haywire. There's an escape pod near you. I can—oh, hang on . . . "

"Fisher!" Mason shouted. "Whatever you did, keep it up! The fleet is falling into disarray!"

"Easier said than done," Fisher said, gritting his teeth. FP was gliding back toward him, holding the core between his teeth. Fisher and his friends had done a lot of damage, but they were badly outnumbered, and the Mechastaceans were closing in.

FP dropped at Fisher's feet, sliding the last few inches. The greenish, grayish folds of the core glinted up at him. Without debating, Fisher pushed FP to the side with his foot and raised his staff high in the air. The Mechastaceans wanted to turn Earth into a concrete-coated nightmare machine while what few humans survived huddled

MECHASTACEAN SHIP CORE

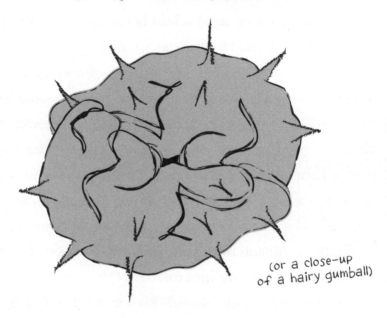

(or a close-up of a hairy gumball)

for shelter among the burnt-out wreckage of their civilization. Fisher gritted his teeth and brought the staff down, crushing the core like a cantaloupe with an audible *splat*. A sickly yellow fluid jetted out, just missing FP. Fisher had to contain the adrenaline surge and the strong desire to let out a barbaric shout of victory.

"Control, this is *Perseus,*" he said after taking a breath. "Primary objective complete."

The Mechastaceans dropped back for a moment.

Amanda turned around, gasping for breath, and still managed to give Fisher a high five that nearly dislocated his shoulder. Alex and Veronica hugged him. In the fractional pause, Fisher looked up at the holographic display.

Three was in a huge space full of conduits and rotating chambers. It looked like it might be a major power generator, or one of the engines. He was covered in machine oil. Half of his clothes had been burned off but he looked unharmed underneath. Scraps of wire and metal hung off him as he tore the room apart piece by piece.

"CURTIS," Fisher said as the Mechastaceans started to come for them again. "You were saying something about an escape pod?"

"Green floor hatch!" CURTIS said. "Look for the green floor hatch!"

Fisher spun around, and spotted the hatch just behind him. More Mechastaceans were swarming the scene, doubly infuriated now that their precious ship's core had been destroyed.

"Whatever you're gonna do, do it NOW!" Amanda screamed as she heaved a pirate aside.

"Okay!" Fisher said. "Follow me!"

There was a large button under a clear cover next to the hatch. Fisher crouched, moved the cover aside, and slammed the button. The hatch popped open with a hiss.

Fisher helped Veronica into the escape hatch first, then

Alex. Alex reached into a belt pouch and handed him a fistful of steel spheres as he went in, winking.

"Amanda!" Fisher said, clenching his hand and feeling all of the orbs activate. "Get in, now!"

Amanda delivered a final right cross, sending a pirate smoking to the floor, turned and dove headfirst into the hatch. Two dozen Mechastaceans advanced on Fisher with murder in their camera eyes.

"Even if you win this battle," one of them screeched over the din, "there are more of us, and they will finish what we began."

"There may be more of you," Fisher said, "but I promise you, there won't be enough."

He scattered the EMP orbs on the floor in front of him, and hopped into the pod, leaving behind the high whine of machinery short-circuiting.

The four kids and the pig huddled together in the tiny space, shaking, still full of adrenaline.

"This is control," Mason said. They could hear cheers in the background. "The fleet is in complete disorder. Ships are veering wildly off course. We're successfully driving them back into space." There was a pause, and Fisher could hear him smile. "You did it, kids. Now just get home."

"Did you hear that? We did it," Veronica whispered, leaning into Fisher. He put his arms around her, nodding, too full of emotions to even speak. They'd defeated the Mechastaceans, but they still had to make sure the Gemini held up their end of the bargain. And what would they do about Three? Recapturing him would prove even harder than fighting the space pirates had been.

But as the escape pod lifted off, Fisher allowed himself a brief moment of rejoicing.

"That we did," Alex said with a smile as large as Ganymede. Amanda ruffled his hair.

"Hey!" CURTIS radioed. "I see ya! Hold on!"

CURTIS wasn't as deft a pilot as Alex, but he was able to guide the *Perseus* up to the escape pod, open the Gemini ship's main hatch, and scoop the pod into its small bay. Amanda kicked the pod's door off and they ran to the bridge full tilt.

"Mason!" Fisher said as they buckled themselves in. "We're back aboard the *Perseus*."

"Glad to hear it!" Mason said. "Is Three secure?"

"Not exactly," Fisher said.

Amanda shook her head. "We can't go back for him."

Alex said, "We *have* to go back for him."

Fisher paused, debating. "CURTIS," he said. "If you're still connected to the flagship's network, could you try to determine his loc . . . " He trailed off as a series of explosions ripped across the big ship's surface, blowing who knew how many tons of debris out into space. A second group of explosions followed, then a third.

"We need to *go*," said Amanda. "Like, right now."

"Right you are," CURTIS said. "My connection to the flagship's computer is down. Pretty sure the whole thing is down, in fact."

"Alex!" Mason's voiced boomed over the comm. "It's too late. You gotta MOVE!"

Alex was already working the controls. He pushed the ship in reverse as fast as it could go. Fisher's restraints bit into his shoulders painfully, and suddenly they were shooting once again into the stars. When they were far enough away to see the whole ship, the *really* big explosions started. The blasts cut across the entire vessel, side to side, up and down. At last, it came apart in thousands of pieces, and Alex turned off the screen to keep the flash from blinding them. When he turned the screen back on, only a debris field remained.

The rest of the fleet was fast fleeing the Earth.

"Come on," said Veronica quietly. "Let's go home."

⇉ CHAPTER 26 ⇇

*The battle for Earth is over. The battle for the chicken wings
at the victory party has only just begun.*

—Hal Torque,
brief sidekick to Vic Daring, Issue #34

Fisher and Alex found their lives endangered once
again—this time by their parents' embrace—when they
disembarked the ship inside the MORONS base. Everyone in the base was on their feet, applauding. Cham-
pagne corks flew through the air. The main screen
was a feed of a hundred TV stations from across the
globe, with news anchors shouting with triumph and
openly crying with happiness as they reported that the
alien menace was retreating into space thanks to an
unknown force's heroic efforts. Even Dr. X seemed to be
smiling, at least a little bit.

"We're bringing you a special report," a news anchor's
voice cut over the din. "A massive invasion fleet has been
turned aside thanks to the heroic efforts of NASA, its
MORONS special operations team, the FBI, and several
world militaries . . . "

"Hmph," Alex said. "And the greatest seventh grade

commando team the world has ever seen."

"You four have saved our species," Agent Mason said, walking up to them, leaning over and handing FP a whole, uncooked potato, which the pig devoured at a rate that would be alarming for anyone who didn't know him. "I know it'd be nice to get the glory you deserve, but I'm afraid we're going to have to keep it quiet, at least for a while. The full story of what happened here has to be delivered to the world carefully. I hope you understand."

"I could use some quiet," Fisher said. "A ton of it, really."

"Hear hear," said Amanda.

"There is still work to be done," Mason said. "That explosion put a huge amount of debris into orbit. The MORONS team will have their hands full dealing with it and they may ask for advice or assistance at some point. For now, you've got another alien species waiting for you."

Fisher rolled his eyes.

"I can't wait. Just be sure to make those modifications to the *Perseus* while we're gone. And get those potato seeds on board."

"Oh," Mason said, "I have a special treat prepared for the Gemini. One of my men will bring it along with you."

"Anything as long as it'll convince them to set sail for a *new* planet," said Amanda.

*　*　*

Nearly every door on the street was wide open, and neighbors were partying and cheering. Cars were stopped in the middle of the street, horns honking, stereos blasting. The technicians and scientists had joined the neighborhood celebration and the carnival sound seemed to extend to every horizon. Spotlights shot into the night sky, and the stars themselves seemed just a little brighter.

The Earth was saved.

Anna and Bee were waiting for Fisher and Alex on the bus. This time, though, there wasn't much left of the bus but its frame, engine, and tires. The Gemini had used up most of their energy in battle, and the drones were eating all the materials they could find.

"Thank you, Fisher Bas," Anna said as crumbs of blue plastic spilled from her lips. "The Mechastaceans have been our enemies for a very long time. It will be years before they can recover from the blow you dealt them."

"I didn't do it for you," Fisher said, trying not to sound too unkind—but not trying too hard. "You plotted to take us over just like they did. Don't think we'll forget that. But . . . you held up your end of the bargain, and we'll hold up ours. Your ship will be returned to you. It will take you directly to your home planet, drop you off, and then fly itself into your sun."

"Well," Bee said, "that is satisfactory, we suppose."

"There's one other thing," Fisher said. He exchanged a look with Alex, who nodded almost imperceptibly. "It's just past midnight now. That makes it Thanksgiving."

He motioned behind him, and an FBI agent rolled up a long cart sporting several covered trays in front of the bus.

"Here we have King of Hollywood's finest in Thanksgiving cuisine," Fisher said, gesturing. "Choice turkey burgers with tangy cranberry mustard, ground beef and relish stuffing, and, of course, spicy pilgrim hat-shaped fries." He took a deep breath. "To new understandings."

There was a momentary pause. Then both Anna and Bee extended their hands, slowly, and in return, Fisher and Alex offered their own. They shook.

Then Fisher and Alex turned and walked away from the alien's bus, for what they could only hope would be the very last time.

"Well," Alex said, letting out a long whistle. "That's that. All's well that ends well, I guess."

"I guess," Fisher said. He spotted Veronica in his mom's garden. "Er, give me a second, okay? I'll meet you inside."

"Hey," Veronica said with a sweet smile. She was leaning against a tree in Fisher's mom's garden. Technically, actually, it was a blade of grass, but Fisher's mom had engineered it to grow to forty feet.

"How's your career as interstellar diplomat?"

"Over, I hope," said Fisher. "Listen, er . . . I never apologized to you. You distrusted the Gemini from the start. I should have listened to you."

She stood, squared up to him, and gently set her hands on his shoulders.

"Why, Fisher," she said, her gentle smile sweet enough that Fisher felt like he needed a dentist, "that's awfully kind of you to say. But there's no need to apologize. I get it."

Fisher felt a very strong impulse, and at long last, he didn't ignore it, push it out of the way, or smother it in doubt. He followed it, placing his right hand on the back of Veronica's neck, . . . gently inclined her head down as he inclined his up. And he kissed her.

The rest of the universe probably continued to exist during that moment, but Fisher didn't really notice.

"Hey! . . . Oh, uh, sorry to interrupt," said Alex. He was holding Amanda's hand. Fisher and Veronica parted, and Fisher made no attempt to quash the likely unquashable grin on his face.

"Don't worry about it," he said. "What's up?"

"I just got a call from Mason at the base," Alex said. "The Mechastacean fleet jumped away a few minutes ago using some sort of faster-than-light technology. They jumped out in a very specific formation, at least when looked at from Earth's perspective. I think you'll want to see this."

He pulled up a picture on his phone. The telescope image showed the many points of light emitted as the ships left the system. The dots lined up in a near-perfect order, just as Alex had said, forming a clear shape when viewed from Earth.

The shape was a 3.

MORONS SI 226445953

ACKNOWLEDGMENTS

The Clone Chronicles rolls on to exciting new places, and we've finally been to space. Or, pardon me, I should spell that properly: *Spaaaaaace.*

Much better.

Thanks as always to Laura and Lexa and everyone at Paper Lantern, and especially to Kamilla, the newest face, and one essential to the creation of this book.

Also thanks to the Egmont crew, and special thanks to new editor Jordan, who's crafted this volume into something sleek and sharp.

To all of my friends, as ever, it's you for whom I write. You who keep my heart dancing after a misstep. And I'm awfully fond of dancing.

That's it for now! I look forward to whatever comes next and I hope you all join me for it. Much fondness to you all.